THE ROMANCE
VOTE

Acclaim for the Cain Casey Saga

The Devil Inside

"Vali's fluid writing style quickly puts the reader at ease, which makes the story and its characters equally easy to get to know and care about. When you find yourself talking out loud to the characters in a book, you know the work is polished and professional, as well as entertaining."—*Family and Friends*

"Not only is *The Devil Inside* a ripping mystery, it's also an intimate character study."—*L-Word Literature*

"*The Devil Inside* is the first of what promises to be a very exciting series…While telling an exciting story that grips the reader, Vali has also fully fleshed out her heroes and villains. *The Devil Inside* is that rarity: a fascinating crime novel which includes a tender love story and leaves the reader with a cliffhanger ending."—*MegaScene*

The Devil Unleashed

"Fast-paced action scenes, intriguing character revelations, and a refreshing approach to the romance thriller genre all make for an enjoyable reading experience in the Big Easy…*The Devil Unleashed* is an engrossing reading experience."—*Midwest Book Review*

Deal With the Devil

"Ali Vali has given her fans another thick, rich thriller…*Deal With the Devil* has wonderful love stories, great sex, and an ample supply of humor. It is an exciting, page turning read that leaves her readers eagerly awaiting the next book in the series."—*Just About Write*

The Devil Be Damned

"Ali Vali excels at creating strong, romantic characters along with her fast paced, sophisticated plots. Her setting, New Orleans, provides just the right blend of immigrants from Mexico, South America and Cuba, along with a city steeped in traditions."—*Just About Write*

Praise for Ali Vali

Carly's Sound

"Vali paints vivid pictures with her words…*Carly's Sound* is a great romance, with some wonderfully hot sex."—*Midwest Book Review*

"It's no surprise that passion is indeed possible a second time around"—*Q Syndicate*

Calling the Dead

"So many writers set stories in New Orleans, but Ali Vali's mystery novels have the authenticity that only a real Big Easy resident could bring…makes for a classic lesbian murder yarn."—*Curve*

Blue Skies

"Vali is skilled at building sexual tension and the sex in this novel flies as high as Berkley's jets. Look for this fast-paced read."—*Just About Write*

Balance of Forces: Toujours Ici

"A stunning addition to the vampire legend, *Balance of Forces: Toujours Ici,* is one that stands apart from the rest."—*Bibliophilic Book Blog*

Visit us at www.boldstrokesbooks.com

By the Author

Carly's Sound

Second Season

Calling the Dead

Blue Skies

Love Match

The Dragon Tree Legacy

The Romance Vote

Forces Series

Balance of Forces: Toujours Ici

Battle of Forces: Sera Toujours

The Cain Casey Saga

The Devil Inside

The Devil Unleashed

Deal with the Devil

The Devil Be Damned

The Devil's Orchard

THE ROMANCE VOTE

by
Ali Vali

2014

THE ROMANCE VOTE

ISBN 13: 978-1-62639-222-9

This Trade Paperback Original Is Published By
Bold Strokes Books, Inc.
P.O. Box 249
Valley Falls, NY 12185

First Edition: December 2014

Credits
Editor: Shelley Thrasher
Production Design: Stacia Seaman
Cover Design by Sheri (graphicartist2020@hotmail.com)

Acknowledgments

Thank you first to Radclyffe for your support and advice, and for giving me such a wonderful home with BSB. You and the rest of the team have been incredible teachers and friends for the last ten years and I look forward to the next twenty.

As I've said before, writing is a solitary art when you're putting pen to page, but once the work is done you realize you're nowhere near finished. The editing process might be feared by some, but I'm so grateful to Shelley Thrasher for all the hard work and time she puts into each book. Her patience, lessons, and red pen are always appreciated, but the thing I value most is Shelley's friendship.

Thank you to the BSB team who all work so hard to bring every book to print. You guys are the best in the business. Thank you to Sheri for always finding the right cover for every book, to the other authors who are always there to offer encouragement, and to my beta readers. How lucky I am to have Connie Ward and Kathi Isserman offer their input from the beginning of every book, so thank you both for keeping me on track.

Thanks to you, the reader. Your support at events and your wonderful emails have meant so much to me. Everything I write is always done with you in mind.

Wow, it seems like literally yesterday that I met a beautiful woman who had me tongue-tied whenever I was around her, but that was thirty years ago. Life has changed as far as jobs, homes, the loss of loved ones, but there has been that one person at my side who keeps me tethered to happiness. Thank you, C, for loving me and for making me laugh. You've always been my definition of pure joy, and with you at my side, I look forward to whatever adventure comes next. You're my best friend, and I love you. *Verdad!*

CHAPTER ONE

"That lying, piece-of-crap, son of a bitch!"

The descriptive rant ran through Christian "Chili" Alexander's head as Garnet Simms sat across from her droning on about what she wanted. It had nothing to do with anyone present at the meeting, or the droner—it just was something that never failed to jump to the forefront of her thoughts when she met with potential clients.

Her father had strung the words together for the first time right after her third birthday, and while she didn't remember the admonishment from her mother, she'd bet even money there had been one for the foul language.

Bruce Alexander had been sitting in front of his new television watching a special about Nixon resigning his office because of Watergate, and he'd been commenting on the president's less-than-honorable exit from the world stage. When Chili's father grew angry about something his hair always appeared darker than usual because his face would get beet red. He usually saved his outrage for football and bullies of any kind, so seeing him get so worked up about this subject had been memorable even at that early age.

Chili had inherited his passionate defense of those things in life that should be fought for and defended, and she'd come out of Harvard with a head full of ideas about how to conquer the world. The only thing missing was an idea of which particular world to conquer. On the way back to her home in New Orleans, a flat tire had stopped her in a little town just east of the city, and it'd been like fate had put that nail in the road.

When she'd walked into the small one-room campaign headquarters of Alvin Millet to use the phone, she'd found her calling. After a slew of internships with PR firms, not of her choosing and most of which included plenty of national political work, she'd been disillusioned with the game of government, but Alvin was different. He was the one candidate Chili had met up to that day vying for a city-council seat that she found had the heart and drive to fairly represent the local constituents. What Alvin didn't have was money or a message, but after a thirty-minute conversation, he did have a new campaign manager. Chili still had a lot to learn after Alvin took his oath of office, but with him she'd discovered the one slice of the world where she could make a difference—politics, but politics of her choosing.

With a few more campaign wins on her resume, the Alexander team had become the most productive and active in the Pellegrin-Morris Consulting Firm, handling campaigns from local to national accounts. Her offices took up two floors of the refurbished building next to the Mississippi River in New Orleans that Huey Pellegrin, the owner, had purchased as a young man. From the moment she stepped off the elevators, she could feel the adrenaline, and that's what made Chili glad to get out of bed in the morning.

Everyone on her staff believed as she did, that their efforts could mold the future into a more decent place one campaign at a time. Every candidate knew that Chili wouldn't represent them if they didn't first sell her on their goals. "If I can't stand the sight of you or believe you, how am I supposed to convince people to vote for you?" That was the first thing she asked every potential client.

Sitting in meetings like this one, she could study the people the potential candidate sent to represent them. Even if the representative could fool her, in her experience idiots attracted idiots, though the hired idiots weren't as slick as the boss. As always, Chili tried to keep anyone from sitting in front of their television and screaming, "That lying, piece-of-crap, son of a bitch."

"You also have to be available to Kathleen and me on a twenty-four seven basis," Garnet said.

The droner then leaned back into the conference-room chair and clicked her red nails together. Garnet was Kathleen Bergeron's chief of staff and campaign manager, since it was a well-known fact that the current state representative and Garnet had met when they were seven. The two now-powerful women had realized even back then that they were better together than on their own. What Kathleen lacked in savvy, Garnet picked up the slack, and what Garnet lacked in people skills, Kathleen the politician handled with polished ease.

"Is that going to be a problem?" Garnet asked.

Chili stared at the media device in the center of the table, acting like she was thinking of a good answer. She'd met dozens of Garnets in her career, and to them the only correct response to that question was, "No problem at all." What the queen bee didn't know, though, was that this was as much an interview for the Bergeron campaign as it was for her. The governor's mansion and who occupied it had been a major pain in Chili's ass for too long for her to take on another moron with delusions of grandeur.

"Everyone knows you want to run. Hell, you've flirted with the idea and been coy in every interview you've given in the last year, and you've raised what some would consider a sizable war chest. Once you announce, had this been any other moment in time, you'd have a considerable advantage, but the reality is you have exactly twenty-four months and four days to convince the constituents of Louisiana that you're the right person to be their governor. Not the right woman, but the right person." She kept her attention on the flat speaker and ignored Garnet and her staff.

"You're currently running nine points behind the sitting governor's handpicked boy, who's raised twelve and a half million more than you, and he's barely begun to work the big-money donors. Considering his party affiliations and their absolute adoration of this guy, gaining ground is going to be about as easy to overcome as climbing Mount Everest in our underwear in the dead of winter."

She never turned her head around when the door behind her opened. "They'll use Roland against you as well." The mention of Kathleen's husband made everyone cringe, but if they feared the truth behind closed doors, the press would murder them. From Chili's experience the good ole boy from the southern part of the state who'd run to the nearest altar when Kathleen had said yes was as opinionated as a group of old women at a quilting bee. That part was fine, but no one had ever been able to stop Roland from borrowing his wife's pulpit when he had something important to say—at least important in the mind of the outspoken and often obnoxious Roland Bergeron. "Rumor on the street is that he'll legislate from the bedroom, and it's picking up steam."

"Do you have any good news?" Kathleen asked, dropping into the seat next to hers and laughing. "I didn't ask Huey to set this meeting up for you to tell me everything that's wrong with me and Roland."

"I have the best possible news." Chili pulled her briefcase closer, took out a packet, and handed it to Kathleen.

"What's this?"

A black fountain pen came out next, from the breast pocket of her jacket. "Your contract."

Kathleen eyed the pen but didn't readily accept it. "That confident?"

"Time wise—today is it. We're already way behind the

competition, so if you want to take a pass on our firm, so be it. Just don't call six months from now expecting miracles."

"Wait a minute, you—" Garnet screamed, smart enough to realize what Chili thought of the job she'd done so far. Garnet stopped when Kathleen put up her hand for silence.

"And if I don't sign, who will you go after next?"

Chili put both the pen and the contract in front of Kathleen, seemingly as relaxed as when she walked in. "No one. This was the only meeting for this particular state race that I've taken. Huey isn't happy with me, but he understands that sometimes it's not about electing the right person, but voting for the least offensive. And before you get your panties in a crack, I wouldn't be here if I thought that about you."

"Will we win?" Kathleen picked up the pen and signed without reading the document. Chili's reputation for winning would close the deal, since Kathleen couldn't take the chance that after she walked out some other campaign would woo Chili, no matter what she'd said.

"Your homework for the moment is to become an expert in health care, coastal restoration, and sugarcane, and pick out a winter-white suit."

"Health care, the coast, and sugarcane I understand, but the shopping trip escapes me."

"The governor takes the oath of office on the steps of the capitol in January. I just thought that with your coloring, winter white would look stunning as you place your hand on the Bible." She stood and shook hands with her new client, then Garnet. "Give me two days, and then we'll meet again to review our action plan. Until then, why not take a few days off somewhere reporter-free? We need to hone your message, so don't make this election harder to win than it has to be by shooting off your mouth without a plan. Make sure Roland gets that part of the lecture, above all others. If he wants to be in charge, he can either run for something or run this campaign into the ground."

"Blunt as always, darling," Kathleen said.

"If you want nice, then hire Fred and his group." She picked up the contract and slid it back into her bag. "I understand he's got a fabulous manner with his clients, especially when he's holding your hand on election night trying to console you. If you have that thin a skin, then not only did I make a mistake handing you that contract, but you've got no business running for garbage collector, much less governor of this state."

"Just start doing what we're paying you for and everyone will be happy," Garnet said when Kathleen's smile disappeared.

"Thanks, Chili," Kathleen added in a nicer tone, after the punch to the gut with what she couldn't deny seemed to have passed.

"Don't thank me yet. You can do that by inviting me to dinner once you're elected. I've heard the cook at the governor's mansion makes a chocolate cake that'll make you forget politics—at least during dessert."

"It's a deal."

CHAPTER TWO

The elevator doors opened and Huey Pellegrin stepped out to what he liked to call his cash-cow floor. "We got it!" Beth Richards held the phone to her ear with one hand and pumped her fist into the air with the other. "We damn well got it."

"They sent Chili into a room full of women, and you had doubts about us getting the contract?" Paul Matherne, Chili's assistant asked, shaking his head. "Get real, Beth. I bet she had them eating out of her hand as soon as she walked in and gave them that killer smile."

Huey laughed at Paul's reasoning and, like everyone standing around him, knew how hard it was to resist Chili's personality. It's what got most of their contracts and why there was hardly any turnover in her department along with a line of folks waiting to come work for her.

Next to Huey stood his daughter Samantha, both smiling at all the backslapping going on. Their hero was still at Mrs. Bergeron's local office, but she'd taken the time to call Huey, and now her staff, so they'd know when to uncork the champagne. It was the thick of campaign season and they'd plucked the juiciest job in the state that year, along with senatorial and house seats in four neighboring states.

Chili had done it again and her team was ready to fight the good fight, every one of them confident of success with her at the helm. Looking at the enthusiasm in each eager face, Huey was sure if Chili asked any of these people to jump off the roof, he'd see them from his window on the way down.

"I see the jungle is going to be hopping today," Samantha said, sweeping an errant lock of blond hair behind her ear. Paul's comment had put a scowl on Samantha's face, and for a moment Huey thought Sam would wind up hitting him for it. "After she gets back they aren't going to get any work done." Sam had stopped close to a cluster of the staff whispering the latest gossip, he guessed, and her mood only darkened further.

"Honey, I think you're the only one in the building who's immune to the Alexander charm. You don't care for Chili much, do you? The rest of these guys seem to have drunk the Kool-Aid when it comes our main attraction."

"Our relationship is just fine, Dad. You just have to pull back a little on the adoration of the golden child. If not, it just goes to her head."

He sighed and shook his head at his only child. He'd warned her about Chili's inability to commit to any woman for more than a month, but Sam seemed to have taken it to a new level. Perhaps she was acting this way for the benefit of his peace of mind, but if she wasn't it'd be a hard lesson if she drove Chili out the door. Even though the firm was Pellegrin and Morris, his partner Chester had passed away suddenly from a heart attack, leaving him the sole proprietor. They were as successful as ever, but he, unlike Sam, understood why. Chili was the reason the clients came, and she had enough wins to guarantee success if she started her own firm.

Their star had been at that point for a couple of years, and if that happened, the "jungle," as his daughter referred to it, would fall silent. He was sure they'd survive, but the loss would definitely affect their bottom line when their slew of clients followed the rainmaker. The business he'd leave Sam would only recover if another Chili walked through the door, but he wasn't foolish enough to think that powerful a lightning bolt would strike twice in one lifetime. They didn't call Chili the poll-vaulter for nothing.

Before he could say anything, the stairwell door opened and out stepped Chili. How she managed the eight floors of stairs every day, a couple of times a day, was beyond him, but it kept her trim and vigorous. He smiled and felt himself relax as he slapped her on the back. The future might be bleak without the golden child, as Sam referred to her, but for now she was here and working for him. That acknowledgment alone calmed him more than any massage he could go out for.

Their relationship had changed from just employer and employee shortly after Chili had come to work for him. She was the only other person he knew, aside from himself and his late wife, who shared their deep love of the political game. For both of them it was a passion whose fire would never go out, and Huey had come to think of her as part of his family.

"Huey, what brings you down to the trenches?" Chili shook his hand, clearly not expecting too many accolades. It wasn't Huey's style, and she wasn't the type of person who needed much praise. Her work and the results were all she needed to stroke her ego. "And you come with such a lovely sidekick."

Samantha rolled her eyes at the comment but remained silent.

"I came to remind you not to be late this Saturday. I expect you on the dock by five, Chili, no excuses." Huey turned and started for the elevator, looking back at her when the doors opened. "One last thing. Congratulations on Bergeron. Good job, kid." He and Sam heard the cheer as they started for the tenth floor.

"What's Saturday?" Paul asked once they made it to Chili's office.

"The Pellegrin-Morris annual duck-hunting trip. There's no better photo op for any politician, Pauly, than to be seen brandishing a firearm. Makes them look tough on crime and strong to the ever-powerful gun lobby." With a flip of a switch the unique boards in the room rolled to fresh, clean white paper.

Chili had always thought better with a pen in her hand, and it was time to start strategizing Kathleen's campaign. Before long, two of the walls in her office would contain the roadmap that would lead the woman who'd just hired them to victory.

"I try to forget that we host that, and I can't believe you're willing to kill some helpless ducks for a photo op."

"Buddy, I'm willing to kill you for a photo op," she joked as she tossed a pile of messages in the trash. Most were from other gubernatorial campaigns looking for some election-day magic. "I don't particularly enjoy spending my weekend in a duck blind freezing my ass off, but this event is nonnegotiable as long as I'm here working for Huey. It's his favorite event that we sponsor, and I don't want to disappoint him. Besides, you know how much he loves dealing with the media."

"Does that mean you may be giving up duck hunting after this election?"

The view out the two walls of solid glass—the churning brown water of the Mississippi River and parts of the port— captured Chili's attention, as it often did. She was silent for so long, Paul turned to go.

"In this business no one would blame me for giving it up," she said, "the duck hunting, that is. But where I come from, you dance with the one who brung you, and Huey was my dance teacher. As long as he's leading the band, I'll be happy to duck hunt. I'm not walking out on him."

"Yeah, but one day Samantha's going to be sitting in the conductor's chair. What then?"

"Then we'll be singing a different tune, but it might still be worth dancing to. You never know until the music strikes up."

❖

The office eventually grew quiet as the staff went home. Already the paper walls were starting to show signs of life, but at this time of day Chili liked to dedicate herself to a different type of research. She scanned the national papers and logged onto the blogs for different candidates and political-action groups to get a feel for what was bothering or exciting people.

It was this attention to detail that gave her the edge very few in her business had, since they usually left it to the peons to troll the net, and inexperience as to what to look for led to huge advantages. That had helped build her winning track record and was also why Huey gave her free rein with all her clients. He had become more of a supervisor when it came to running the business. The combination worked well and was why he had included her in some of the most important moments of his life.

She took her reading glasses off and leaned back in the antique wooden desk chair, remembering one of those days. Of all the people he could've asked, including a large extended family, Huey had put Chili at the top of his list.

Early December, the previous year

"Chili, you about ready to go?" Huey was putting on his jacket, patting his chest to make sure the invitations were in the pocket.

The office on the eighth floor was quiet, the employees having gone home early to start their Christmas shopping since this year they'd most likely be working. Their days were quieter now with no active campaigns under way, none of any consequence, but they'd recently picked up something that was more like a training exercise.

Politics was never dormant, even without special elections. The hopefuls always had their eye on the next office and were quietly polling to see what their odds were. Then on the other side of that coin, the incumbents were making plans and hatching schemes to hang on to their shreds of power at any cost, even if it was by their fingernails.

She walked to the elevator still wondering why Huey had offered her his second ticket to the important event he was attending that night. "Are you sure you don't want to take your sister?"

"You know how Sam feels about her aunt, so quit your griping and get in. You don't have some hot date, do you?"

"I'm not seeing anyone at the moment, so I have no other place to be."

"What happened to Candy?"

She laughed as she stared at the ceiling of the slow-moving elevator. "Her name wasn't Candy."

"It should've been. Any woman seen in public dressed like your last romantic interest should have a pole at the ready somewhere in the vicinity, and the dancer name to go with it."

The doors opened to an empty lobby with Huey and Chester's picture hanging near the entrance. "I take it you didn't approve."

"I call her and every single one of them you date Candy for a reason, Chili."

She locked up behind him and put her arm around his shoulder as she guided him to her car. "Lay it on me. I can't wait."

"She's just a little piece of fluff. You know, like a piece of candy you have to help digest a big meal. In the big scheme of things it's the meal you remember, not the fluff you have afterward." He pointed his finger in her face to stop her laughter. "You think it's funny, but you can't make it through life on fluff."

"What if the main course makes me fat and lazy, though? What would you do then?"

"Retire happy knowing someone out there cared about you past the morning."

They talked shop as Chili drove them to the Tulane campus,

where they found a parking spot near their final destination, but it couldn't be declared a miracle. December graduations, while important, were much smaller affairs than their May counterparts.

Samantha Pellegrin, Chili knew, had excelled in her course work and finished early so she could accept her father's job offer. While the campaign they were about to start was small compared to most, it would be a good opportunity for her to learn from both Huey and Chili. This type of education, Huey had told her, would teach her more than Tulane could.

Not shy, they sat on the first row and talked to the people around them as well as the ones who stopped by to congratulate Huey. Every time one of them did, Chili had to hide her amusement at his aggravation.

"Why do people do that?" he asked.

"Maybe they think her great accomplishments are because of genetics, and since her mother isn't here to take credit for your daughter's brilliance, they have to make do. We all know that's where Sam got her brains and good looks."

"Have you always been this sassy?" he asked with affection. Lillie Pellegrin, from everything Chili had read about her and had heard from Huey, had been brilliant and would've had a legendary reputation in the business by now, but she'd lost her battle to a bad heart when Sam was four. Her loss had left Huey in turn heartbroken, and time hadn't made him want to move on with anyone else. Aside from a few dinner dates that revolved around work, Huey's whole world was Sam and the business.

"Sorry, I couldn't resist, and I could tell by how you keep patting the picture in your coat pocket that you're thinking about her. If I had the power to grant you one wish, Huey, she'd be sitting right next to you."

"Lillie would've loved this."

"Until she saw who the guest speaker is tonight. From what you've told me about her, she might have been tempted to heckle him during his speech. Hell, I might do that in her honor."

"Yeah, Senator Billy Fudge was one of our first clients, actually."

"You represented that pompous ass?" Chili turned in her seat with the same sense of shock that would have registered if he'd suddenly told her they were representing David Duke for Grand Wizard of the Klan.

"I realize one of the things you pride yourself on is your gut when it comes to people and what they hold in their heart." He stopped to shake hands with another well-wisher. "I had a pretty good track record on that myself until Billy."

"He must've put up a hell of a show if he fooled you that badly."

"Not only me but Lillie as well. He ran, got himself elected, and once he won, he changed his party affiliation two weeks after he got to Washington." Huey shook his head in apparent disgust. "It went downhill from there. His record on the environment and women's rights made me want to start a recall petition on the ass, but damn if he doesn't squeak out a win election after election. Makes you wonder about the intelligence of the voters in this state."

They both faced the stage as the proceedings started. The deans and the president of the university came out and took their seats on the stage as the graduates filed in from the back. There was the usual pomp and circumstance, and after Senator Fudge gave the commencement speech, the valedictorian got up and gave another talk.

After all the things Huey had done to change the face of politics, Chili could tell from the way his chest puffed up that his proudest moment was when Samantha rose and walked to the podium. Samantha Pellegrin wasn't only beautiful, but she was also one of the brightest people Chili had ever met, and having her around the office starting Monday was going to be *interesting*.

"In closing," Sam said five minutes later, "my class

and I would like to offer our thanks to the professors who so generously gave of themselves. Our time here will leave us with fond memories and a good foundation to build on. As my father loves to say, the future belongs to those who fight for it. If you want it to reflect what you want, stand up and be heard. History isn't made by the silent. Thank you all."

As soon as the graduates collected their caps off the ground, Sam came over and fell into Huey's arms. "Your mother would've loved to have seen you tonight, baby." He wiped his eyes and pulled her tighter. "You did great."

"Thanks, Daddy." Sam kissed Huey's cheek and wiped away his tears. "Thanks for coming, Chili," Sam said when Huey let her go.

"Congratulations." Chili gave her not-as-vigorous a hug as Huey, then held out a small box she'd fished out of her jacket pocket. "I hope you don't mind, but I picked up something to help you remember the day."

Sam ripped the box open like a woman who loved getting gifts and then just stood still when she opened it. "Your dad told me that your grandparents gave your mom a string of pearls the day she graduated, and it was her favorite piece of jewelry since she was wearing it the day she met this guy," Chili said, pointing to Huey. "I'm sure if she'd been here today, she would've continued that tradition."

"This is beautiful." Sam kissed her on the cheek and Chili's ears got hot, which made Huey's eyebrows go up, but he didn't say anything. "Could you help me?" Sam asked as she pulled the strand out and handed it to Chili.

"I'm glad I guessed right." With a quiet click Chili fastened the clasp and let the strand rest around Sam's neck. Her gift really stood out against the black of the graduation gown. "The pearls look great on you."

Huey thrust a camera at Chili, and the picture of them smiling ended up on his desk.

❖

The memory was one of Chili's favorite. She'd be forever grateful that he'd included her in something so special. It wasn't as if she didn't have a family she loved dearly, but her parents didn't share the same love for politics as she and Huey did. They had a passion for the game that not only ran deep, but it ran in the same vein. Chili hated to think where they'd be if Huey was her complete opposite when it came to the voting booth.

She clicked on the webpage of Steven Fajil, Kathleen's opponent, and laughed at the sperm picture that popped up, or at least that's what she liked to call it. He was in his early forties, had a beautiful wife, and there on her lap sat the proof that his swimmers worked: a boy who appeared to be around three and his baby sister, who Chili remembered reading had been born just four months prior. It made a touching scene and would work well out on the campaign trail as Steven tried to pound Kathleen into the pavement with his message. That their current and very popular governor loved this guy and would be singing his praises at every campaign stop wouldn't hurt once they started in earnest.

Before she could scroll down to see if his bullet points of information had changed any, her phone rang.

"Alexander."

"Still at the office?"

While the question was asked with what Chili guessed was annoyance, all she did was prop her feet on her desk. "Yes. I'm still at the office because I'm still working."

"Of course you're still working. For the all-knowing Alexander to quit before midnight would be a sin. If you decide to knock off early though, I'll make it worth your while."

"I still have numbers to run."

"Or nipples to squeeze. Your choice, lover." And with that the line went dead.

CHAPTER THREE

December, the previous year

"We've been hired by Virgil Emery for a run for the Louisiana State Senate. In case you've been suffering from a severe head injury that's prohibited you from watching or listening to any type of news outlet, you know that the sitting senator from this district will start serving his twenty-year sentence in a federal penitentiary for tax evasion and money laundering at the end of the month. Mighty impressive for someone who only got himself reelected recently."

Chili stood in the middle of her office with her main team around her, as well as a number of newbies hoping to move to the inner circle of a bigger campaign the next year. Virgil Emery was a training job, but he was about to be overwhelmed by Chili's staffers, who wanted something larger than the Louisiana State Senate. "The first thing we'll have to overcome besides his polling numbers is how to make Virgil sound cool."

"What's his middle name?" Paul asked.

"Michael," Chili said as she wrote the name Virgil on the board.

"V. Michael Emery sounds like a guy I'd vote for, boss."

"Michael is his father's name." She kept writing, filling the board with his latest numbers and his opponent's strengths and weaknesses. So far he had a lot more items on the strength side of the list since he'd served two terms in the Louisiana State House.

From the sound of flipping paper, Chili could tell everyone in the room was reading the file she'd handed out as they walked in. She finished her notes and turned around to find every face buried in the file except one.

"So what's wrong with that?" Sam asked, causing everyone to shut their files and lean back in their seats in what seemed to be anticipation.

"Michael Emery was a dock worker who spent most of his paycheck in the bar close to his job, beat his wife, and abandoned his family when his wee little boy Virgil was only three. From that fateful day, daddy dearest never looked back and never paid a cent of child support, forcing Virgil's 'sainted mother,'" Chili made air quotes, "his words not mine, into working three crappy jobs to keep them in Spam as a treat. All that added up to a pitiful income that paid for an apartment you wouldn't let your dog live in, and so much peanut butter the man still has acne. Virgil would no more go by V. Michael Emery than he would tattoo 'Kick Me' on his ass."

It usually only took one time for someone to receive this lecture so that they'd do their homework before asking uninformed questions, even if it was the boss's daughter asking them. Chili crammed the lecture down their throats, since it was especially aggravating when she did all the homework and they only had to read the damn file she'd handed out.

"Point taken." Samantha crossed her legs first, then her arms over her chest. "If it would make you feel any better, you can slap me now and make me sit in the corner. I'll even wear a funny hat if you have one."

"I didn't say all that to embarrass you, Miss Pellegrin." She laughed when Sam cocked her head to the side and smirked. "Well, maybe just a little. It's better that it happen here, where any mistakes will be pointed out and then forgotten, than in public or, better yet, in front of our client. There's no harm done, and from now on just read the file when I throw out a more-than-obvious hint like telling you Michael is his father's name."

"What's your suggestion then when it comes to his name?" Sam asked.

"Dolly, get with the art department and tell them simple. I'm thinking French blue, block letters with white and blue piping around the edges. Just *Emery* at the top and *Senate* at the bottom. If they want, tell them to do another one with 'for' in the middle of the page, at an angle." Instead of answering, Chili started working down her to-do list and handing out assignments to her seasoned staff.

"You got it. I called and made an appointment this morning before this meeting," Dolly said.

"Beth, get with Jamie and tell him I'll need about a week of his time. Also, he has to be on standby in case our opponent throws any curves toward the end of the run. I need you to work on five scripts to begin with, and I want them to be manly. The environment shot should be on or near a duck blind in camo, and make sure his shotgun isn't shiny new." She wrote down a few more notes in her planner and finally looked up. "The rest of you, the usual workup for the media and mailers, so get cracking. Put together the shell with what's bothering the voters most these days and how Virgil's going to turn it all around for them. I'm meeting him in an hour to go over some other things, but our first tentative package has to be done by the end of the week."

"You didn't answer my question about the name," Sam said as soon as they were alone in the office.

"I will, but first tell me what your suggestion is." She held her finger up and grabbed her car keys. "Better yet, come with me, and after you meet Virgil you can let me know what your thoughts on the subject are."

"Why can't I do that now?"

"You could, but why take a chance on being wrong twice in

one day?" Chili opened the door for her and laughed when she could see how much her teasing was aggravating Sam. "Impress me with what you learned with that political-science degree you got."

"What would you like to know?"

"How to run a campaign from beginning to end? Let's start with that." Chili turned the radio off and pulled into traffic.

Sam looked at Chili to see if she was serious. For the last three years of her life all she'd heard when she had dinner with her father was how amazing Chili Alexander was, and just how brilliant and exciting she made every day at work. After hearing it over and over again, she'd overloaded her schedule in her last semester so she could come in at the beginning of this campaign as one of the newbies. She'd had plenty of chances to meet the campaign guru since Chili had come to work for her father, but not too many one-on-ones like this.

So far all she knew about Chili was the obvious, like how good she was at her job and that she was incredibly good-looking. The good-looking part had hit her in the gut the day they'd met and was hard to ignore, especially now when Chili was smiling and waiting for her to answer the question she'd thrown out. It was also amazing how quickly her little crush had died under a few minutes of full-on Chili.

She hesitated to give Chili what she wanted, thinking that perhaps this was another instance Chili was going to have a laugh at her expense. When she sat silently for the entire drive, Chili pulled into an empty parking space of a huge Lexus dealership but hesitated before getting out.

"You don't have to be so skittish around me, Sam. In the next year all I'm going to do is try to help you reach a point where you can hang your portrait in the lobby and move upstairs with Huey without feeling like it's just been handed to you."

"Why do you think I wouldn't want my future handed to me on a silver tray?"

"You're the daughter of Lillie and Huey Pellegrin, so call it a guess. The business is going to be yours unless you have a burning desire to open a shoe store or something, but the tenth floor will just be an empty prize if you don't work for it, don't you think?"

"So you asked to see how much I don't know?" Sam asked, and gripped the armrest hard. The next year would be long if all Chili did was throw one verbal dart after another at her expense.

"I asked because I was interested in how you'll process a campaign, but if you're going to act like I'm going to jump you every time you make a comment, then it's going to make for some long days," Chili said as if reading her mind. "No matter what, you've got the job, but don't let the rest of the staff come to disrespect you by folding at the first mistake. One day you'll be signing their paychecks, and you want them to be as proud of the work as they are now."

"You don't know me enough to accuse me of being spoiled."

"True, but if you were a potential client, I would've dropped you by now."

"For?" she asked, the flush she could feel rising from her chest becoming uncomfortable.

"For acting like you're unteachable. People who act like that are either smarter than everyone else or they don't care to learn from their mistakes. Today's the day you prove you're cut out for this or you're not."

"Why? Because I'm not tripping over myself trying to prove I'm your number-one groupie, or is it that I can't come up with a good enough answer to prove I'm nothing but a smart-ass who's spoiled beyond redemption in the eyes of the great Chili Alexander?"

"You don't have to prove anything to me, Miss Pellegrin. The one who needs convincing is you."

Chili got out of the car and let Sam get her own door this time around. She laughed when Sam glanced up and saw the name Emery on the building and snapped her fingers, obviously realizing why the name sounded so familiar. "Is he in? Could you tell him Chili Alexander and Samantha Pellegrin are here to see him?" Chili asked the receptionist.

Virgil came out in a suit that was anything but senatorial and a tie so bright orange Chili didn't take her sunglasses off.

"Huey called me last night and told me you're on the job. From what my people tell me, you're the best," Virgil said, so loud that Chili figured Huey had also told him she suffered from hearing loss.

Before she could get her hand all the way up to shake Virgil's, Sam grabbed her arm and pulled her to the bathroom. "This is who we're going to try to get elected to the Senate?" she asked in a hiss.

"If he doesn't fire us before we get started."

"He's a car salesman," Sam said, like Chili didn't realize where they were and who they were talking about. "Is this another joke at my expense?"

"Maybe next year around April Fools' Day I'll think of something this elaborate to punk you with, but Virgil's for real. There's got to be something about him that your father found appealing. I haven't figured out what that is yet, since I couldn't attend the interview." Chili squeezed Sam's fingers and smiled. "Anything else before Virgil calls 911 and has the police escort us off the premises?"

They walked out, and Virgil was standing there with a woman whose hair was so blond it made Chili forget about Virgil's orange tie. Sam turned her head to Chili when she heard the soft "shit" at the sight of the couple.

"Chili." The blonde opened her arms and stepped closer until her hands were locked behind Chili's neck. "I couldn't believe it when Virgil told me that your firm was on board with us."

"Paula, what are you doing here?" Chili stepped back so quickly she bumped into Sam. "I want you to meet Samantha

Pellegrin," Chili said with a tight smile, standing slightly behind Sam after she finally broke Paula's grip on her.

"Your firm will be in charge of the overall picture, but Virgil needed a campaign manager for the day-to-day things, so he hired me for that."

"Fabulous," Chili said in a way that made her wish she'd wake up and find that this was all a bad dream. That would explain Virgil's tie and Paula. "This is going to be a short election cycle, considering the circumstances, so we need to get started. If you don't mind, Paula, Sam and I need Mr. Emery for a couple of hours."

"Way ahead of you. We're set up in the boardroom," Paula said.

"And you two," Virgil said in his booming voice as he put his arms around both her and Sam, "we'll be working together, so you all call me Virgil."

"Who's Paula?" Sam asked in a whisper as they made their way to their seats once they'd wriggled out of Virgil's embrace.

"Not right now, okay?" They stepped into the conference room and saw a few signs already on the table that Paula had obviously drawn up. None of them looked like anything Chili would put in her yard, even with the promise of a new car off Virgil's lot. "First thing we need to do is get you a headquarters location that isn't in this building. We have a few places that are available and visible, so they'll be easy to find. That'll be advantageous when we start asking for volunteers to put out the signs and such that our art department will come up with," she said, pushing all Paula's work aside.

"I figure this place is easy to find," Virgil said. "In case you missed it on the way in, it's got my name on the building in big letters." He laughed in a way that his shoulders shook.

"It'll also remind people that you're a car salesman. Honest profession, I'm sure, but it's right up there with lawyer and snake-oil salesman when it comes to polling, so we're moving out of here today. Before we make any other big decisions, though, why don't you tell me why you want to get elected to the Senate in Baton Rouge, Mr. Emery?"

"It's Virgil, remember, and I've already told Mr. Pellegrin why."

"Mr. Pellegrin isn't here, Sam and I are, so let's hear it," Chili said, and placed her briefcase on the edge of the conference table but didn't sit down.

"I love to fish and hunt, Ms. Alexander, and one day I'm going to take my kids out there and there ain't going to be one blessed thing living in those marshes and swamps. These may be luxury cars I sell, but I grew up simple and having to make my own way, so I want better for my kids. I want a seat at the table to make sure the yahoos who run this state can't use any money set aside for coastal erosion for anything else. They keep doing that and the goddamn Mississippi is going to be flowing through Canal Street if the right storm comes along." He slammed his fist on the table and leaned over it to get closer to her. "That's the best answer I got."

"Anything else?"

"We got a whole lot of crime on the streets as well, so I want to do something so decent folk can go out without the fear of getting shot in their neighborhood." Virgil slammed his fist down again and appeared ready to connect with her eye if she asked anything else. They'd have to work on the short temper, but the conviction in Virgil's voice was something you couldn't coach.

"Let's go shopping, Virgil, and please call me Chili from here on out. And remember, under no circumstances do you use the word *goddamn* in public again until after the election."

"Just tell me where the building is and I'll have Paula go over there and set it up."

"My staff will take care of everything on that end. That's not what we're shopping for." Chili took her car keys out and took a deep breath. "We need to update your look a bit and get some new ties."

"What's wrong with my ties? My mother gave me this tie." Virgil held it up like it was something he was willing to use to kill her with if she tried to take it away from him.

"I'm sure next Mother's Day your mama will love to see you wearing that when you take her out to dinner, but from now until Election Day I don't want to see it again." As Chili spoke she unknotted it and took it off him. She folded it carefully and placed it on the conference table. "You can argue with me if you want, but I want you to remember that the guy whose job you want is going to jail wearing a lovely orange jumpsuit that screams criminal. Orange is something that reminds people what's wrong with the political system and the crooks running the show."

"I see," Virgil said, and unbuttoned the top of his shirt.

"If this is going to work you have to trust me, Virgil. You might not like everything I have to say, but I'll never lie to you, and I'll never tell you anything unless I have a stack of paper and numbers to prove my point." Chili waited for his list of reasons why he didn't want to do what she was suggesting, but all Virgil did was nod.

For the rest of the afternoon until Rubenstein Brothers Clothing Store for Men closed, Sam watched in amazement as Virgil allowed Chili to pick out a new wardrobe for him. As she stood next to the tie rack with Chili while Virgil tried on one more suit, she noticed just how long Chili's fingers were. Chili had strong-appearing hands that weren't adorned with any jewelry, and it was easy to imagine what they'd feel like anywhere on her body.

"I can't believe he's being so docile about this," Sam said, and found a red silk tie that made the white shirt in Chili's hand pop.

"He wants to win, so I think he's going to make it easy on

us and listen. This doesn't always happen, believe me, but maybe we lucked out this time around."

"I had no idea this was part of our job."

"Surprisingly, this is one of the most important things about our job. Undeniably any candidate's message is the most important thing, but if you don't want to look at the messenger because he looks like a hick who sells cars with bad taste in clothes, then it's pointless. To get it right you have to balance style with content without going overboard. If that happens, your guy comes off too slick and that turns off voters faster than a Day-Glo-orange tie. You shouldn't have any problem with this part."

Sam pulled out a few more ties and placed them with the shirts Chili had pulled out. "Why do you think so?" Despite their rocky start, the rest of their day had actually been fun.

"Because you look beautiful, and you do every time I see you."

The comment left Sam stunned even after Chili walked off in the direction of the dressing room with what they'd chosen. Spending this kind of time with Chili was going to be interesting if she kept up the compliments.

Sam had a feeling that Chili was the kind of person who noticed a lot of things, but more importantly a lot of others noticed plenty about Chili as well. Chili's height combined with the light-brown hair that was graying around the ears and her light-blue eyes she was sure were a lethal combination when she was on the hunt for company.

However, she doubted that was what was in Paula's head every time her eyes cut to Chili. She didn't care for how Paula sat back and watched Chili the whole time, and companionship had nothing to do with it. If she had to define the smoldering in Paula's eyes, it was lust.

Those two had a history, and Sam was determined to find out what it was without having to ask her father. He always said the secret to this job was to ask as little as possible and find out as much on your own as you could. Too many questions were at times your downfall because they revealed your plans in the answers others had to give you.

"Well, what do you all think?" Virgil asked when he stepped out of the dressing room. The navy-blue pinstriped suit, along with the white shirt and red tie, made him appear like a different person. Even if all Virgil ever did with his life was sell cars, you'd feel better about signing on the dotted line sitting across from this guy than you would if he'd still been wearing the loud neckwear and tan suit that was slightly too small. "Think I need some new shoes to go with this rig?"

Chili and Sam gazed down at his black alligator boots and shook their heads at the same time. "No, but the big diamond Rolex has to go," Chili said, and handed him a simple wristwatch with a leather band. "Now you look like the senator people are going to put their faith in."

"You really think so?" Virgil asked as he studied his reflection.

"Almost, but as soon as we go over a few more things you can bank on it."

"Isn't this dishonest, though, even if my wife will be thrilled? She's been after me forever to change my look, but real men don't care about stuff like that." Virgil held his arms out and let them drop. "Without your help I'd still look like a hick."

"Let me share with you the most important wisdom I learned from my mentor when it came to politicians. After the votes have been counted and you and your wife start looking for an apartment in Baton Rouge, the clothes and a good haircut can make you someone people are more likely to sit and listen to, and that'll win you the seat. What I can't change is what your beliefs are and how you express your passion about them. That comes from the part of you no new tie and suit can dress up enough to get elected. Your convictions are going to keep you honest and in favor with the people who'll put their trust in you."

"I think I'm going to like you," Virgil said as he slapped Chili on the back.

"Don't worry. By the end you're going to love me," Chili said.

When the manager of the store came with the bill, Sam pulled Chili off to the side again and whispered what she thought was an important point. "You do realize that he's twenty points down in the latest polls, right?"

"And here I thought you didn't read anything in the report," Chili said with a smile.

"I'd like to think I learn from my mistakes."

"Don't we all," Chili said and laughed, but she stopped abruptly when Paula stepped into her personal space, pushing Sam aside.

"Chili," Paula said, and wrapped her hand around Chili's bicep in a way that reminded Sam of an octopus getting ready to devour some helpless fish. "How about we get together over drinks tonight and talk strategy?"

"I'm sorry. I have a dinner meeting with Huey tonight to set our schedule for the next couple of months. Have Virgil go over the position papers we sent him and make sure he gets his numbers right." Chili's smile had faded, and she almost seemed to strain to break Paula's grip. Sam had never seen someone so blatantly go after someone like they were a piece of meat and she was a hungry piranha.

"Did I hear my name and some sort of homework?" Virgil asked.

"I want you to become an information wonk overnight, Virgil."

"Shucks. Doesn't the state have enough of those already?"

"A bumper crop, but you're going to be much different than all that." Chili stepped closer to him and straightened his tie. "There's being a wonk who spits numbers out like a Gatling gun, and then there's being one who's also a successful car salesman.

You've got the charm to make them sign on the dotted line, and we're going to use that to get you elected."

"You're pretty good at that too, so what's next then?"

"Get to know the facts as a way to arm yourself, and while you're doing that I'm going to get to know your opponent. You'll build your strengths, and I'll find the weakness in the other guy so you can deliver enough blows to even out your numbers a bit." Chili accepted a bag from the salesman and gave it to Virgil. "Only keep one thing in mind."

"What's that?" Virgil asked, but wasn't referring to the bag in his hand.

"If your opponent is even halfway decent, and considering his polling numbers at the moment he is, his people are doing the same thing we are, with great success. That means no more than one drink when you're in public, no speeding, I don't care what the problem or emergency, and when you attend church on Sunday, if I catch you sitting in the first row of pews I'll personally kick your ass. There's nothing more aggravating than a politician who goes for the most visible seat in the church, because even if you do it every Sunday, everyone is going to see it as a cheap photo-op."

"Anything else?" Virgil asked as he peeked in the bag.

"Plenty, but I don't want to overwhelm you on the first day." Chili tapped on the side of the bag so Virgil would open it all the way. When he pulled out the pink tie with little race cars on it that Sam had picked out but that Paula had thrown out of the bunch he'd bought, Sam smiled at Chili. "A gift from Sam and me for Election Night. The women will love it, but the race cars will keep anyone from thinking you're too sensitive."

"I think I'm going to like you a lot," Virgil said, and put the tie back in the bag carefully.

"See, that's what separates you from the competition, Virgil. You're smart," Chili said, and laughed. "Read the files, and we'll see you first thing in the morning."

"Chili, I expect you'll make some time for me as well. There's so much to cover and so many hours in the day. Maybe dinner or drinks, if not tonight sometime this week?" Paula said, and ran her finger from Chili's shoulder to her hand. "Not that much time has passed that you don't remember what a great team we make."

"I'll make a point of having Chili's assistant review her schedule, and he'll get back to you," Sam said, and opened the door for Chili.

Sam followed her out and didn't say anything to break the silence on the way back. She hesitated when Chili stopped in front of the office and put the car in park but didn't turn the ignition off. "Good job today, Sam," Chili finally said, but didn't look at her.

"It's only four. You're taking off already? I have a lot of stuff to ask you about."

"Does it count that I was here until ten last night?" Chili finally gazed in her direction. "It won't take you long to get the political fever that makes this job the center of the universe, but even less time to figure out that sometimes it just makes you sick. I'm on bullshit overload, and I'd like nothing better than to sit somewhere quiet and have a drink."

"If you're in a rush to meet someone, then I'm sorry I'm taking up so much of your time. Next time I'll drive my own car so you won't have to be burdened with having to bring me back."

"Did I say this was a burden?" Chili said each word slowly and looked at her like Sam had lost her mind, which she was questioning herself about. "The first rule of this game is to never assume anything. The second rule to memorize is it's no place for spoiled little girls." Chili gripped the steering wheel and her nose flared. "I never took you for one so I didn't consider I'd have to mention it. Take tonight to decide if this is too much for you. Virgil Emery wants to be anointed a state senator, and it's our job to get that done. In the realm of all things he's going to have marginal power, but to him and the other peacocks in Baton Rouge it means the world."

"I didn't realize you held our clients in such contempt," Sam said, and opened the door as she felt her anger rise, but she had about as much control over it as she did the weather. "My father and most of my professors said the day that happens it's time to contemplate retirement."

"Well, hey, if your father and professors said it, then it must be true. You did, after all, graduate at the top of your class, so it's only reasonable to assume that even though it's your first day you can already read minds and do it better. Great—have at it. What the hell do I know?"

"What in the hell's wrong with you?" Sam said, and slammed the door closed again since she didn't want anyone to hear her screaming. "I was making a point, so you don't need to be an asshole about it."

"I'm not being an asshole. What I am is tired and don't need any more curve balls than I've had thrown at me today."

"You want to tell me what's up with you and Paula, since I assume that's the curve ball you're talking about."

"There you go assuming again, and just because you're the boss's daughter doesn't mean everything's your business, which in this case it isn't, if you didn't understand what I just said."

"If I'm going to be forced to work with you, then it is most certainly my business. I want to know your head is in the game and not on some woman's ass." The moment the words left her mouth Sam knew she was way over the line.

"Get out of the car," Chili said succinctly. "Now," she added with a little heat when Sam didn't move.

Sam opened the door and stood with it open, getting ready to apologize when Chili put it in drive and left. *Great, just great. At least my first day will be memorable.*

CHAPTER FOUR

The door closed with the momentum of the car moving forward once Sam had done as Chili had asked. "Fuck," she said as she concentrated on the road, refusing to look back to make sure Sam was all right.

She hadn't meant to take her mood out on Sam, but running into Paula was the last thing she'd expected, and the fact that she'd have to work with her was more than she'd planned for the coming weeks. Their history had started during the second campaign she'd handled on her own after going to work for Huey. The lieutenant governor's race had pitted their client, the son of a prominent New Orleans political family, against an aging country singer who'd been a one-hit wonder. Huey had trusted her even though she didn't have that much experience, and he'd been the one who'd introduced her to Paula at their first strategy meeting.

It had taken Paula exactly two days of blitz flirting and outright come-ons before Chili found herself with her pants around her ankles in the bathroom of the campaign headquarters after a long day out campaigning with their client. The sex had been good at first, but Paula was one of those women who you figured out for a psycho leech the moment the haze of lust wore off. When Chili broke it off, things had gotten ugly. It was the only campaign she'd ever come close to being fired from after the show Paula put on the morning after their last night together.

Only Huey intervening on her behalf had saved her job with the campaign and her reputation.

Now they ran into each other occasionally, and when they did, Paula acted as if they'd never broken up and if she tried hard enough Chili would just fall back into the role of the obedient puppy who rolled over and played dead on command. Those passes were easy enough to ignore, since they didn't happen often, but working closely with her on another campaign was going to be like sixty days of constant root-canal work.

"And don't forget about Sam in the middle of all that," Chili reminded herself when she turned onto the road that would take her over the levee and to the shores of Lake Pontchartrain. Her three-bedroom houseboat was permanently docked on the water in a marina made for such structures. It was about as far away as she could get from the hassles of the office that was only a fifteen-minute drive.

The damn thing had cost her a fortune, but she hadn't had anything else to spend the money on, and it was better than saving for triple-bypass surgery from the stress she accumulated at work. Here the only things causing a ruckus were the crickets that chirped along the shoreline.

She stopped and got her mail and flipped through the envelopes as she made her way to the end. Most of her neighbors were weekenders who seldom made an appearance more than a couple of days a month, so she never looked up until she reached her gangplank. The wall of television sets went on as soon as she unlocked the door, but tonight she was more interested in the ones recapping the weekend games. C-SPAN would have to wait until she could open a beer.

"Guess what happened to me today?" Dale Alexander, Chili's brother asked as he stepped out of the kitchen with two beers in his hand. He laughed when the mail shot in his direction and Chili gasped from the surprise.

❖

Sam watched the taillights of Chili's American sedan disappear around the corner and balled her fingers into a fist to fight the urge to call her and apologize. The last comment she'd made was sarcastic and totally unprofessional, but her mouth had engaged before her brain could filter the words, so all she could do was go home and worry about what tomorrow would bring.

"Are you free for dinner?" she asked action-reporter Maria Poplin when the need to call someone won out.

"What's wrong?" Maria asked, the sounds of the studio behind her as they set up for what Sam knew was the five o'clock news. "It's your first day so it can't be that bad."

Maria had been a senior when Sam had started attending Tulane, and they'd struck up a friendship when Sam made an appointment with her world-history professor and got his teaching assistant instead. Their stint as lovers had been brief since their spark in that arena was nonexistent, but they enjoyed spending time together, so Maria had become one of her closest friends.

"I insulted my boss and got thrown out of the car."

"Huey must've lost his mind to get that kind of reaction out of you." The noise died away from Maria's end and Sam figured she'd escaped to her office.

"Daddy isn't my boss at the moment."

"Uh-oh," Maria said and laughed. "Who'd he put you with?"

"Chili the Great." She glanced back where Chili had turned and hoped she'd return for the apology she was due.

"What the hell did you tell her? I've interviewed her a few times, and she never loses her cool no matter how obnoxious my questions get."

"How special for you then," she said, her sarcasm in full force again.

"I'm on at five and six, so after that I'll be happy to tell you how special I am and listen to your sorry tale."

"Sorry I'm being such a bitch, but it's been a long day." She took a deep breath to control herself from taking out her mood on Maria. "Did you want to call and ask Danielle to join us, or should I?"

"She's in Miami pitching their bid for the carnival celebration they're having in the Cuban section of town."

"I thought the whole city is the Cuban section?"

"From what I understand, it is, but they don't like to admit it. All I know is she's eating, drinking, and smoking cigars on a nightly basis—a habit she'd better lose somewhere along the way before she gets back here." Sam heard a muffled yell from Maria's end, then someone banging on something she guessed was her door. "Hang in there and we'll head over to Lucy's after I tell the citizens of our fair city what the hell is going on."

"Thanks, and be good."

Chili wasn't coming back so Sam turned and headed to her car. If she wasn't the boss's daughter, she doubted she'd be allowed in the building in the morning, but unfortunately for her, she wasn't only allowed, but expected. "Way to go, Sam," she mumbled as she walked. If tomorrow went any better it'd end up in a catfight.

❖

"Don't you ever call first?" Chili asked as she picked up her mail. "One of these days you're going to kill me from the shock, and I'll make it my personal mission of my afterlife to haunt you on a twenty-four-hour basis."

"I'd be afraid, but knowing you, you'd spend your time scaring the snot out of plenty of politicians out there, leaving me in the clear." Dale continued to wipe his hands on her dish towel and smiled. "Besides, considering the pitiful pile of stuff you have in that fridge, you should thank me for coming over here and saving you from certain death if you eat anything in there."

"It might be a cure for some terrible disease, so be careful if you throw anything out."

"You're past the cure stage for anything," he said, pointing behind him toward the kitchen, "and onto weapons of mass destruction. If you wrap it carefully and really try, I'm sure you could get a military contract."

"So you're making anthrax soup?" She dropped the mail, along with everything in her pockets, in the silver dish she kept by the door.

"Hell no. I double-bagged all that shit and hauled it the curb. We got some especially good rib eyes at work, so I thought I'd come over and share."

Chili accepted the beer he handed her and sat at the small table by the glass doors to watch him work. Dale was as comfortable in the kitchen as she was in the middle of a campaign, and sometimes she envied him that. His job very rarely followed him home and kept him up nights. The place he owned in the French Quarter was closed for dinner on Mondays, so, on his day off, she often found him cooking for her when she got home.

"Thank you, and I'm sure Mom thanks you."

"I don't cook for you because I think you're not taking care of yourself, which clearly you're not. I do it to spend time with you."

She could hear the tinge of hurt in Dale's voice and noticed the slump of his shoulders as he stirred something on the stove. Her life moved at a million miles an hour sometimes, so Dale always made the effort to see her, and that he still did it so enthusiastically made her sigh at how bad she was at personal relationships. She should've looped the block and gone back and talked to Sam.

"What's the long face for?" Dale asked as he sat across from her.

"First tell me what happened to you today."

"The governor was in town and stopped in for lunch." Dale took a long swig from his beer around a smile.

"Did you spit in his soup as a personal favor to me?" She laughed along with him.

"No, but I wished I knew his list of food allergies. The pompous ass told me to tell you hello for him, and to let you know there were no hard feelings." He got them a couple more beers and pointed her to the outdoor kitchen on her back deck that she'd had installed for him. "I had to remind myself that I'm in the hospitality business."

"It still sounds like you had the better day." Her mouth watered when he put the two large steaks on the grill and they immediately sizzled. "Sam started today."

"I thought you were looking forward to that."

"Yeah." She squeezed the back of her neck in an effort to loosen the tight muscles that the sight of Paula had knotted from there down to her shoulders. "Huey and I thought we'd start her on something easy that probably has no chance of succeeding."

"A loser campaign is your idea of a good thing?" Dale asked as he shook his head and laughed. "That's a sweet kid, Chili. Maybe you shouldn't disillusion her right off, since according to your friend the governor, that's coming in the next election when his handpicked boy takes over for him."

"We all have them, and there isn't a lot going on that'll keep us in town." She'd picked the label off the bottle a tiny piece at a time and wadded all that into a tight ball. "Everything was going okay until we met with our client and his supposed campaign manager."

"Which are who and who?"

"Virgil Emery and Paula Stern." Simply saying that bitch's name made her stomach churn.

"We'll get back to Paula the asshole in a minute, but how does Sam fit into all this?"

She threw her label at his head. "And how do you know Sam has anything to do with anything?"

"Because if it was all about Paula you would've cursed, screamed, and gotten over it by now. I haven't heard your talent in using the word 'fuck' in every way imaginable, so there's got to be something else."

"You should sell the restaurant and open up a detective agency."

"I would, but I look like a pervert in a trench coat."

She laughed and told him the story of her day as he plated their food and poured the wine. "I shouldn't have lost my cool, but it's like she saw a raw nerve and danced a tango on it in her Pradas."

"So what happens now?" He put a pie in the oven before he joined her.

"If Huey fires me for tossing his daughter out of my car, I can retire and spend my days watching C-SPAN with Dad and helping Mom find you a nice young lady to marry."

"Keep it up and I'll spit in your dessert. Huey would fire Sam before he goes anywhere near you."

"I'll apologize in the morning and see where that gets me."

"Make it sincere or it'll be a long few months with the car salesman."

They spent the rest of dinner talking about old times and planning their annual fishing trip. She treated Dale to a couple of trips a year to thank him for the meals he prepared, and he always picked fishing. Aside from getting her all to himself for a few days to reminisce about their childhood, he probably did it so he could brag about the fish he served in the restaurant to his staff and the patrons.

With their meal finished they drank the rest of the wine as the pie cooled, and he took out a large file and laid it on the table between them. "You want to review the books?" Dale asked.

"Do I ever want to review the books?" It was cool out, but

the dying logs of oak and mesquite Dale had used were still putting out heat.

"When I embezzle and run off with your half of the place, don't complain."

"Can you pay yourself and everyone else?"

"Comfortably," he said as he poured out the last bit of wine evenly between them.

"Then I don't need to see the books. Hell, if I can't trust you I might as well shoot myself in the foot."

"Don't you mean to say, shoot yourself in the head?"

"And miss the next governor's race? I'm more likely to shoot someone else than myself, especially when I run into people like Paula."

"If you do decide to use her for target practice, we're doing well enough to bail you out," he said as they tapped their glasses together. "Did you put the twenty-fifth in your calendar? It's the folks' anniversary, and Mom invited a few friends."

"If she has some blind dates in the making, can I put hot sauce in her martini?"

"She said she learned her lesson after the last time."

"Which is what she said the time before that. Don't you remember, or have the onion fumes finally melted something in your brain?"

"True, she did promise before, but she'll be too busy telling Dad's side of the family that every single one of them was wrong about her and how long their marriage would last, including the evil bitch that is her mother-in-law."

She laughed before she shoved a piece of pie in her mouth. "That's true, but Granny might be safe if Huey tosses me out to teach me a lesson on manners. Then Mom will have something else to talk about."

"You've known Sam since she was in high school, so stop with the gloomy talk and practice your apology. Since the day you met her you've gone on and on about how smart, cute, and pleasant she is. One little mishap on her first day isn't going to change your opinion of her. All you have to do now is make sure she doesn't change her mind about you before you get a chance to act on your crush."

"I'm too old to have a crush," she said, and promptly stopped talking because she sounded so whiny.

"Sure you are. Remember who you're talking to. I promise I won't tell anyone, but it's cute as hell to me."

"Thanks, old wise one, and leave the pie," she said when he got up and kissed the top of her head. "Did you call a cab?"

"I always do, since the best part of growing older with you is the booze. Are you going to be okay?"

"One more piece of your coconut custard, and I can even face Paula, Virgil, and Sam all at the same time."

"Come by this week for lunch and give me an update." He kissed her head again and waved as he headed out.

For two people who'd grown up together with nothing in common aside from their parents, it amazed her that Dale had become her closest friend and sounding board. They still had nothing in common, but she found him a good listener because his approach to politics was the same as most of the general public. He voted, and that's where his commitment ended. It wasn't that most people didn't care; it was that following the day-to-day world of government was sometimes as exciting as watching gum harden on the sidewalk.

"Let's see what fresh hell happens tomorrow, because today I totally fucked up."

❖

"I see," Maria Poplin said, after taking a sip of her Cosmopolitan.

"What?" Sam's body warmed from the scotch she'd ordered. Relaxing this way could become addicting considering the career she was embarking on, so she'd have to watch her alcohol intake. The way her father described it, his days sometimes blended from one political event to the next, and the only thing they had in common aside from the bullshit was cheap liquor.

"You like her, don't you?"

"Some investigative reporter you are," Sam said, but couldn't quite take her eyes off her glass. "My dad raves about her all the time, and because I'm his daughter, I get to see the reports of what she does. Chili knows how to win without having to sell her soul to the devil, and I've been really excited about working with her."

"If I were interviewing you for a job, you'd be hired, but you didn't answer my question." Maria put her hand over Sam's. "You don't realize you're doing it, but you talk about her a lot, and you only do that when you're interested in someone."

"Chili isn't exactly someone you like, Maria, and even if I was that delusional, she seems commitment-phobic. Sam doesn't do players."

"You just have to go about it differently than you usually do." Maria held up two fingers as their waiter neared.

"I have a usual way of doing things?"

"Don't sit there and act like you don't have people tripping over themselves to ask you out. Up to now you haven't had to be selective because all you're interested in is a good time. Even if that's all you've wanted, there's been a queue of folks willing to do anything from line dancing to skydiving while handling poisonous snakes to get you to say yes. I guess they figure a few rattler bites is worth getting you between the sheets once someone, preferably you, sucks the venom out of them."

Sam finished her third drink and accepted the fourth, even though it'd guarantee a hangover in the morning. "I'm beginning to believe you make up all that shit on TV as you go along. It's shocking no one's sued you for libel."

"Did you take up a crack habit I don't know about that's

made you forget the year we were roommates?" Maria held her by the chin so she could look her in the eyes. "All those hopefuls coming by with their sad puppy faces wanting to know when you'd call and asking if I'd put in a good word. I should've said yes, for a fee, and whittled those college loans down."

"You make me sound like a slut," Sam said as the waiter came with two more drinks to add to their fourth round. "Is it two-for-one all of a sudden?"

"The two gentlemen at the bar wanted to treat you," the waiter said, and pointed to the two guys he was talking about. "Anything else I can get you ladies?"

"Could you send these back?" Maria asked, pushing both glasses to the edge of the table.

"You'd turn down free drinks?" the waiter asked but picked them up anyway.

"Do we look like Cosmo whores to you or something?" Sam asked, and the guy took a step back. "You can tell them our parents taught us to never accept anything from strangers. And before they take that as a challenge to come over and introduce themselves—we'd like to remain strangers to them."

"As my father the prosecutor used to say, the state rests," Maria said to Sam once they were alone again and laughed.

"It could've been you they were interested in, you know."

"Yes. I'm sure the back of my head is sexy as hell, since that's the only view they have of me. Face it, Ms. Samantha, you're a beautiful woman that people find desirable. If you in turn find Chili desirable, it's a win-win for you."

"Even if I agree with you, after seeing Paula, I'm in no way Chili's type. And before you become as obnoxious as the guys heading this way, I don't agree with you."

"Mind if we join you?" the first guy asked.

"Once you see that we're harmless, you'll see we didn't drop anything in those drinks we sent over," his friend said.

"We weren't afraid of a roofie. We're simply not interested.

I live with someone, but I can't speak for my friend the female impersonator. He can usually be persuaded, but only if you'll form a human naked train with him as the caboose." Maria rested her chin on the palm of her hand and smiled.

"No fucking way you're a guy," the first guy said to Sam.

"You've never heard of RuPaul's second cousin, Marvelous Marvin? He's on the show all the time," Maria said with a straight face. "Come on, live a little and broaden your horizons. You can finally check having a ten-inch penis shoved up your ass off your bucket list," her smiled widened, "and if you give him twenty minutes, you both can."

"Sorry to bother you." The men ran back to the bar so fast they came close to taking out the table next to them.

"Marvelous Marvin? Where do you come up with this stuff?"

"If you can't bluff you'll never make it very far as an investigative reporter." Maria paid their bill and hailed a cab for them. "The other lesson I've learned is that a burger will soak up all this booze so you won't resemble a sick raccoon in the morning."

"With wisdom like that, you should go into politics."

"It's much more fun digging up dirt on politicians than being one, and if they dug up my past there you'd be. You don't want to be the six o'clock lead in a story, do you?"

"No, but after my first day, I'm regretting I didn't go with the dream to become a vet I had when I was six." Sam stumbled a little getting out of the cab but caught herself on the back of Maria's skirt before she fell. "Then the only slimy things I'd have to deal with were snakes."

"You'll have plenty of those in your line of work—trust me." Maria put her arm around her waist and led her inside the Camellia Grill. "Give yourself a chance, Sam, and you'll catch the fever soon enough."

"And Chili and the harem I'm sure we'll run into along the way?"

"I can't tell you what to do about that, but make sure you know the consequences before you do anything at all."

"What are you talking about?" Sam pressed her palms around the glass of ice water the waiter put down and enjoyed the cold.

"You were right about one thing when it comes to Chili. She's good at what she does, Sam, really good. Put all the personal stuff aside and think about what kind of relationship you want to have with her, professional and otherwise." Maria stopped as the food arrived. "You stick your toe in that pool to see what the fuss is about, and she'll move on."

"That's obvious. Paula proved that," she said before taking a huge bite of her burger. Suddenly she was ravenous.

"No, girlfriend, she'll move on from the firm, and she'll have plenty of offers if she does."

Sam licked ketchup off her thumb and laughed. "I'm not that hideous in bed."

"I know that, but Chili wouldn't disrespect your father or you that way. At least that's the impression I get of her. If she leaves, the firm will survive, but understand the rainmaker Chili is and what a drought would do to your bottom line."

"Did you sleep with her? You sound like her biggest fan."

"Actually I'm more a fan of yours."

CHAPTER FIVE

I'm sorry," Sam and Chili said simultaneously the next morning in the parking lot.

"Why are you apologizing?" Sam asked, her sunglasses firmly in place despite the dreary, overcast morning. Maria had lied about the burger and fries absorbing all the alcohol. "I was the butthead yesterday."

"I was being polite," Chili said, and pointed out the diner a few buildings over. "Besides, it's not often one of the newbies has the power to fire me."

"Shouldn't you be more polite then?" Sam followed, not ready to go into work yet. "Like saying I'm not a butthead, or at least not agreeing with me."

"How about instead of deciding whether or not you're a butthead, we agree the day ended at Rubenstein's yesterday. Whatever came after that didn't happen. Deal?" Chili put her hand out as they stopped on the sidewalk. Sam stared at it for a long time before taking it.

"What's the catch?" Sam asked now, not letting go.

"I don't think they serve fresh seafood, but you look like you could use some eggs. Late night?"

"Not what I meant, but eggs sound good."

Chili smiled, held the door for her, and picked the table by the window. The waitress handed only Sam a menu. "You're not getting anything?"

"She knows I'm a creature of habit about some things, but the chili omelet's their specialty."

Sam put her hand over her stomach and shook her head. "I don't think I could handle chili today."

"Maybe it's plain eggs they named after me."

"Is your ego always this healthy?" Sam pointed to something on the menu and nodded toward the waitress.

"Actually I'm a shy introvert."

Sam came close to snorting coffee out of her nose. "Yeah, I can see that. Do you have a bridge to sell me later?"

"Maybe, so try to behave, smart stuff."

"Do you want to talk about yesterday at all?"

"If you mean Virgil and anything to do with his campaign, sure," Chili said, and took a sip of coffee while she organized her thoughts. All the relaxation from her dinner with Dale had drained from her body and been replaced with tension in Sam's presence.

"I was more interested in why you act like Paula is the original Typhoid Mary. Do you two have a history?"

"I met Paula a few years back before I came to work for your father."

Sam stared at her, blinking slowly, but didn't say anything until it was clear Chili didn't intend to elaborate. "And? There's got to be more to it than that."

"There might be more to it than that...or there might not. You need to learn that your private life should stay private. At least I'm going to keep mine that way."

Sam shut her mouth so her lips formed a thin line as the waitress poured more coffee. "Wouldn't it be faster to just say it's none of my business?"

"If I did that, you'd think I was being an ass again," she said, and put a finger up when Sam inhaled sharply as if ready to hit her with a hailstorm of words. "You don't need to deny you think I'm an asshole. I figured that out on my own. I said it because, even though we're not running for office, someone's always looking for an advantage. Share everything about yourself and there'll always be someone who'll eventually try to use it against you."

"Is that what happened with Paula?"

She had to give Sam credit, she'd do a bulldog proud, but with a face like Sam's and an ass that'd stop traffic, most people would cut her some slack. "It's none of your business, Sam, so drop it."

"You realize I won't let this go, right?"

"If you're that curious, have at it and ask around. Believe me, it won't be that hard a search, and when you've got your answer it might be enough to get me fired, since you have that power." She dropped a twenty on the table and accepted the bag the waitress held out. "Maybe once you do show me the door, you can explain where in the hell I went wrong."

"What do you mean?"

"Granted, I called you down yesterday, but this is more than that. Believe it or not, I was really looking forward to working with you on a full-time basis. You've always reminded me a lot of your father, and I wanted to help you make your path. After yesterday and now, I see you don't like me much, but you don't know me well enough to feel that strongly about it, so I must've done something."

"Wait," Sam said when Chili reached the door. "It was a simple question, and if you don't want to answer, then don't. You don't have to run out on me."

"I've got an early meeting so I'll eat on the way. Don't worry. You don't need to apologize again, and I'm late. Think about what I said and I'll see you later."

Chili had forgotten to get coffee to go, but she was damned if she was going back in there, so she walked briskly to her car and called her office. "Paul, remember I'm in Baton Rouge this morning, but it shouldn't take long. Patch through anyone who can't wait. If not, I'll see you in a couple of hours."

"Paula Stern has called for you three times already. You want me to patch her through?"

"Do you think you'd look rugged with your front teeth missing?"

"Fair question, boss, and I'll tell Ms. Stern you've moved to the Amazon to live with the pygmies. They were looking for someone tall to pick the high-hanging fruit, and the clothes-optional way of life made you jump at the chance."

"Remember to make an appointment with a mental-health professional and stay out of trouble until I get back."

❖

The Louisiana state capital was full of people running around as if they held the answer to the state's woes so it was important for them to get where they were going, no matter if they plowed you down to do it. Chili had enough contacts to become a successful lobbyist either here or in Washington, but her bullshit limit was too low to put up with these jackasses for long. Her side of the political game was too exciting to quit for three times the money she was making now.

"Did you come to help me or to encourage electric-shock treatments again?" a man asked as he covered her eyes with his hands.

The move reminded her of elementary school, but State Senator Theodore Rooster Roberts was anything but simple. Rooster was one of the savviest people she'd met in this line of work, and he had only two years left to his term. The only thing that'd finally unseated him was the term limits he'd helped to pass a few years prior.

"I'm going to demand it if you called me because you've got

your eye on some other office." She turned around and hugged Rooster, who enthusiastically returned her embrace.

"Can you blame me?" Rooster kept his arm around her shoulder as they walked in the direction of his office. "You've got this bug as bad as I do, so don't give me all that shit about quitting. Both of us will quit when we're old and senile. Hell, even then we'll have better ideas than most of the jackasses around here."

Rooster's office had a beautiful view of the Mississippi River and part of the city. His seniority had gotten him the space that was even larger than the governor's office, and the asshole in that position at times couldn't stand that fact. Rooster's large desk sat between two large windows, and over his chair on the wall hung the largest wild boar Chili had ever seen. The thing's name changed every few years, depending on who'd pissed Rooster off, and at the moment the pig shared the governor's first and middle names.

"What's on your mind?" Chili asked as she sat at the small conference table on the other side of the room, since that's where the coffee service was set up.

"Don't make me beg." Rooster sat heavily across from her and accepted the cup she'd prepared for him. "Tell me what the public has on its mind."

"Right now you're running six points behind the incumbent if the election were held tomorrow. That's not an impossible number to make up, but he's got a war chest bigger than one of those barges out there. It's enough money to paint you or anyone who dares run against him as a wild-spending, God-hating, flag-burning liberal the second you announce."

"Any good news in that bag of tricks?" Rooster leaned his head back and covered his face with his hands. "I promised Carla I'd only consider it if we could avoid a mud fest." Carla Roberts was Rooster's second wife, but the only reason the young, gorgeous twenty-six-year-old had caught the sixty-two-year-old Rooster's eye was because his sainted wife of thirty years had lost her battle to cancer. It'd taken Rooster four years after that to crack a smile, but Carla had completely changed his life after Rooster's daughter Gabby had introduced the two of them.

"If you want this, really want it, you're going to have to fling a little slop yourself. I know it's not your style, and it hasn't been necessary in your district since everyone who lives there thinks you're the anointed one, but negative campaigning has a way of sticking. Once they slime you it's hard to get rid of the stink, so you might as well warn Carla now."

The door opened as Chili was talking, but she finished when she saw who it was.

"Might as well warn me about what? I assume you two are talking about me," Carla said as she kissed Chili on the cheek before heading to Rooster. "Come on, keep talking. That's why I'm here."

"Your husband has had a long and successful career here despite being a Democrat in a very red state, and he's about to retire from state politics. If you two have Washington-type ambitions it's not impossible, but don't expect the cakewalk it's been up to now to get yourself elected."

"You don't think Rooster's got some good left in him?" Carla asked as she took her husband's hand.

"People across the state are going to take one look at you and think Rooster's got a whole bunch left in him, I'd imagine, but I want you both to go into this with eyes wide open." Rooster laughed and Carla joined in as Chili took out the report she'd compiled and gave them each a copy. "These are the results of the polls we took, as well as how I believe they'll come after you. You've got a good team, and I think, if done right, you'll give Blow Hard a run he won't soon forget."

"How about you, Chili? Isn't it time you got involved on the policy side?" Rooster asked. "I can offer you a good gig with a view as pretty as this one."

"I'm not ready to beat my head against the wall yet, so stick with Charlie. He's good people," she said of Rooster's chief of staff. Usually state senators didn't have large staffs, but Rooster had the money to go along with his charm and good looks.

"That's all you got for me?" Rooster asked as she stood to go.

"Thursday of this week you've been invited to speak to the oilmen's group in New Orleans, followed by the chamber of commerce for lunch. I put some speech ideas in the back. Later this month you're talking to the largest faith-based organization in North Louisiana. These people meet quarterly in Alexandria, and they love to hear preaching from the pulpit as to who to vote for, so deliver the speech I wrote word for word. No ad-libbing, Rooster, I mean it. Carla, make sure not to miss that one, and both of you try to look as conservative as possible."

"You're never this specific, so what's up?" Rooster asked as he thumbed to the back of his folder.

"Good things come to those who show surprise and awe at the stupidity of others when the time comes. Word for word, don't forget that."

Chili took her time walking back to the car and thought about the rest of her day. "Unfortunately there's nothing else to keep me away from Sam and the human octopus," she said to herself as she reached the parking lot. "Both of them seem hell-bent on making me relive my embarrassment."

❖

"Have you met her?" Sam asked Chili's assistant Paul.

"Paula Stern, you mean?"

"That's who we're talking about. Chili told me to ask you."

Paul's hands rose slowly from his keyboard, and he just as slowly swiveled his chair in her direction. "Chili Alexander told *you* to ask *me* about Paula? Seriously?"

"That's why I'm here talking to you," she said, crossing her legs in an effort to exude calm.

"Are you sure about that? I ask, because knowing Chili the way I do—she'd rather be strapped to the statue in Jackson Square buck naked and beaten than talk about Paula." He stared at her as if trying to see through her game. "Do you mind if I call her before we go on with this?"

"Okay, technically she didn't say specifically to talk to you, but you know the story, so let's hear it."

"I also know that setting my ass on fire would probably really hurt, but I don't want to try and prove myself right. Why do you want to know so badly anyway?"

She slid off Paul's desk and pulled her skirt down. "Curiosity, nothing more, and if you're not going to indulge me, then don't mention this to Chili, okay?"

"It's our little secret," Paul said as he held up his crossed fingers.

The shit was going to tell Chili the first chance he got, she thought as she stepped into Chili's office. She'd visited here so many times in the middle of campaigns, when it was hard not to get caught up in the frenzy, and often daydreamed during her classes of spending her career doing the same thing. The enjoyment would be short-lived if coming to work meant navigating a minefield littered with eggshells.

"Did you get a chance to swing by Virgil's new headquarters?" Dolly Larson, one of Chili's team, asked as she put up the new artwork on Chili's wall.

"Was I supposed to? Chili didn't mention it."

"I'm sure she'd appreciate you checking it out before she gets back. Paula called and said they're almost set up, though I'm not sure what that means since we did everything yesterday."

Dolly handed Sam a slip of paper with an address and waved as she left.

"Please let Chili know where I am if she beats me back," she said to Paul.

She took the opportunity to escape for a while and noticed the location Chili had picked was a few blocks from the other candidate in the race. Since she passed that headquarters first, she slowed and took a look at their handiwork. The signage out front was passable, and a few cars sat in the parking lot, which Sam guessed belonged to volunteers. Overall it appeared normal in a "this is our headquarters" kind of way, which is why Virgil's place really stood out.

The parking lot at Virgil's was decorated with the flag streamers usually found only on car lots, and over the main entrance she couldn't miss two large wooden cutouts of rifles crossed with little explosions coming from the barrels. That alone was bizarre enough, but an American flag was pinned to the butts, along with a sign that read GOD BLESS AMERICA. The only thing missing was a statue of Jesus holding a vote-for-Virgil sign.

"Where are you?" she asked when Chili answered her phone. No way was she getting out of the car since Maria and her crew were setting up to shoot a segment for what Sam guessed was the noon news. It had to be an either extremely juicy story or truly bizarre to get Maria interested, and Virgil had delivered in grand fashion, so she couldn't blame her friend for covering this.

"About twenty minutes from the office. Is there a problem?"

Sam held her phone up and snapped a picture. "Can you pull over and look at the text I just sent?"

"Give me a minute." Sam slouched in her seat, praying Maria wouldn't notice her. "Are you fucking kidding me? Is that Maria Poplin the action reporter next to that news van?" Chili asked, her voice booming through the phone.

"The one and only, and from the looks of it, the cameraman's trying to get her to stop laughing before they go on air." That was an easy call since she'd been around Maria enough to know what she was like with a case of the giggles.

"Slowly drive away and meet me at the office. If Virgil goes out and gives Maria any more ammunition to go with the flag and guns, he's on his own."

Sam waited outside until Chili arrived and didn't interrupt the telephone conversation Chili was having as they stepped into the elevator. "Did you get drunk and decide to punk me last night?" she asked someone. "Shit."

Beth Richards was holding her phone to her ear and shaking her head when they got off at their floor. "You know me better than that. Come on. That place didn't have any of that crap when we left last night."

"Get Virgil on the phone and tell him if he talks to Maria 'I'm waiting for my big break' Poplin with that circus in the background, I quit." Chili appeared ready to either throw her phone at something or hit someone. "And if he decides to defy that suggestion, tell him to put that goddamn ugly tie back on so he'll complete the redneck-asshole image he's shooting for."

"Does this happen often?" Sam asked when Chili stood in the middle of her office, breathing so hard Sam figured she'd faint at any moment.

"I'll tell you after we fix this, okay?"

Sam could hear Beth in the background, and it sounded as if Virgil was in the building. Chili had turned on the television, which showed Maria talking as she headed for the door. Thankfully it was locked, but she knocked hard enough to rattle the glass.

"Chili, Mr. Emery's on line one for you," Paul said through the intercom.

Sam couldn't tell if Virgil was still a client, since all Chili said was "uh-huh" twelve times before she gently put the phone down and sat. "Let's wait until our action-reporter friend has finished and cleared out before heading back over there and redecorating." Beth had stepped back in and nodded at everything Chili said.

"I'm sorry I doubted you, and I trust that you, Sam, and some of the others will make the changes necessary to make it look like we're running for the state senate and not state clown."

"I should tell you—" Sam said, but Chili's phone rang again and she answered it.

"I'm not doing live with you again, and before you start, you know exactly why. I just learned from experience, so we can tape it or nothing."

Sam thought back to what Maria had said about not rattling Chili's demeanor, but maybe that wasn't the entire truth. She had to come clean about Maria now or suffer the temper she'd just seen from her new boss.

"Sam, you ready?" Beth asked, but Chili was still on the phone.

"Sure," she said as she walked away, glancing back at Chili a few times. "Crazy day, huh?"

"And it ain't over yet, kid," Beth said as they all crowded into the elevator.

Sam hoped Beth's words weren't a curse. Her relationship with Chili was already shaky enough.

❖

Chili headed to Virgil's house before she had to face the gloating face of Maria Poplin. She thought that was the safest place for the come-to-Jesus talk they had to have before the situation became the funny story people told at cocktail parties for years to come. All she knew so far was the guns and fanfare were courtesy of Paula, since Virgil was running in a conservative, affluent, and religious part of the state. That usually translated into white, gun-loving, rich, somewhat pious older men who loved and lived for the opportunity to vote.

Except for the age, in a way that described Virgil, who, like everyone on his block, had a flagpole dead-center in his front yard. The flag blowing in the wind looked brand-new, but the pole had been there as long as the house, so no one could accuse him of pandering his patriotism because of an election.

"Welcome to our home," the beautiful blond woman who answered the door said as she held out her hand. "I'm Candy Emery."

"Chili Alexander, ma'am." She tried not to think of Huey and his nickname for all her dates as she shook Candy's hand. "It's a pleasure, and thank you for having me over."

"After hearing Paula and Virgil talk about you so much, I feel like we're friends."

"That'll be true by the time this process is done." She followed Candy to the gorgeous study Virgil had in the back corner of the house. The mahogany-paneled walls, antique desk, and book-lined shelves behind it bore no resemblance to the life Virgil seemed to lead outside this room.

"I'll leave you to talk," Candy said.

"Actually, Mrs. Emery, I'd like it very much if you'd stay. Before every election process I tell every couple the same thing. Virgil is running for office, but he's not the only one this campaign will affect, so I'd like your input."

She learned more about Virgil in the next fifteen minutes than she'd planned, but it was what she needed to right his ship. Candy wasn't some fluff Virgil had married to better his image; she was a member of one of the richest families in Louisiana. The former debutante had met Virgil in college, and they'd been devoted to each other ever since.

"There's a way to go about these things, and I'm not so inflexible as to try to bend you into something you're not. What I can't and won't do is butt heads with someone set on going in the exact opposite direction of all our advice for the entire campaign. If that's what you want, I'm okay with it, but the firm will pull back and do your polling and back-room stuff if you want to let Ms. Stern handle your campaign."

Virgil and Candy agreed on how to proceed, so Chili drove to the station to keep her appointment with Maria. She didn't totally dislike Maria, but she had a way of barraging you with rapid-fire questions so your answers at times seemed to get jumbled.

"Good to see you again," Maria said as she sat down.

"Sure." Chili exhaled in an effort to relax.

"How are things?" Maria stood as the techs attached her mike and earwig. "We haven't spoken in a while, and that's my loss. Who knew you had so many exciting things happening in your life."

Chili smiled at her and decided not to fall for Maria's usual bullshit. She liked Maria, despite her profession, and she never outright resented her for it. From what she'd seen of Maria's work she was mostly balanced and fair, but like everyone in the news business, sometimes she let ratings matter more than anything like the truth. Right now she was also wired minus the earwig, and when any microphone was in the vicinity, she had to assume it was live.

"You're right," Chili said, and the crew stopped talking. "I just got a new gym membership and I'm happy with my choice. Other than that, not much exciting to report."

"Have you driven by Virgil's place? Come on, that's exciting. Where'd you find assault rifles that big?"

"Save the questions for later, or we won't have anything to talk about."

"Always the pragmatic one," Maria said as she sat next to her. The crew returned to their gossip, and Maria laughed at what she apparently assumed was Chili's stubbornness.

The interview went as expected, with the scene at Virgil's that afternoon playing in the background and Chili talking only about Virgil's stance on the different topics the campaign centered on. It didn't take long for Maria to move on to other things, including the governor's and senate race, which was a few years in the future, and those answers Chili kept fairly neutral. Maria was done after that.

"Do you mind if I have Sam on next week?"

It was a strange question, considering Sam wasn't on a leash that she knew of. "You'd have to call her and see if she's interested. She doesn't need my permission."

"I ask because she'll probably want your blessing, and I promise if you give it I'll stick to the theme of the next generation of Pellegrin king-makers."

"I'll run it by her and have her call you."

"Thanks," Maria said, and shook her hand.

Now all she had to do was meet with Paula and explain her future role with Virgil's campaign. After that she could go home and peel her skin off and enjoy a beer. She'd called Paula on the way to the studio, and her ex had sounded excited to finally get that drink date she'd been after. Chili had chosen the Petroleum Club, since the clientele would hopefully make Paula think before creating a scene. That was no guarantee, but the possibility of future loss of business might motivate Paula to behave. Nothing turned off potential clients more than channeling a demonic psychopath in public.

"Chili, how the hell are you doing?" the host asked when she stepped off the elevator on the thirtieth floor. The view of the river and city were spectacular up here, and she stopped to look out the windows even though she'd been here often.

"Older by the day, Manny."

"You must be getting bat-shit crazy too, if you're here to meet Paula Stern. Do you want to come up with a code word for the bartender?"

"If he hears the phrase 'I'm going to kill you slowly and with a lot of pain,' tell him to develop a sudden hearing loss. After the last few days I might not be kidding."

Paula was already at the bar watching the interview Chili had just finished, now airing on the five o'clock news. The portion

Maria had shot at Virgil's stayed on longer than Chili would've liked, but that story would soon be put in its grave, where Chili would bury it under fifty feet of good press. She stood back and waited for the segment to end, wanting to watch it without Paula breathing in her ear.

"You want to explain why I was escorted from Virgil's headquarters this afternoon?" Paula asked, skipping her usual syrupy welcome when Chili sat next to her.

"So we could take down the tacky shit and burn it behind the building. What exactly was going through your brain when you came up with that genius idea?"

"Virgil's got to play to the people who vote and will elect him, especially in an election cycle where folks will be as motivated to go to the polls as they will to step in dog shit."

"A fourth of his district falls in the New Orleans city limits," she said slowly, so the words would sink into Paula's martini-soaked head. "The last time they voted for someone with giant gun cutouts in front of their building, Abraham Lincoln was president, and they voted for the other guy in that election too. Starting tomorrow Sam will keep the schedule, and if you need anything, go through her or Beth from our office. Your only job will be to make sure Virgil knows where he's supposed to be—that's it."

"I'd rather go through you, and I'm not a glorified secretary. Virgil hired me as his manager, and you're going to have to accept it. Hell, we're already getting press," Paula said as she pointed to the television.

"True. If there were a show centered around the funniest campaigns and the idiots involved with them, we would've won today. Press like that is like celebrating that your guy's the only one running with syphilis. It sets him apart and gets you plenty of airtime, but not in a good way."

"I'll promise to be good if you promise to stop pretending to hate the sight of me." Paula snaked her arm around her shoulder and pulled her closer. "You can't have forgotten the heat between us. I sure haven't."

"I have a long memory when it comes to you," Chili said, and Paula tightened her hold, "because the screaming show you put on is still vividly fresh in my mind. And in case you're wondering, it always will be."

"Don't exaggerate, baby. It's obnoxious."

"I'm not exaggerating. I'm being kind." Chili stopped to take a large drink from the beer the bartender had poured and put in front of her before quickly retreating as far away from them as possible without actually leaving the building. "I'll continue my giving ways by trying to move forward from the disaster the last time we worked together turned out to be. This campaign is short, but it's important to Virgil, so you need to remember it's about him and not you."

"What the fuck is that supposed to mean?" Paula asked, saying each word slowly and not exactly in her inside voice.

Chili understood the tone since she'd been on the receiving end more than once. Paula was like a dormant volcano rumbling to life. When she blew it was a spectacular show that made for a good story, if you were on the sidelines looking on and not in the path of the lava flow.

"I met with Virgil and Candy today, and they both signed off on the new distribution of duties." Paula's fingers dug into Chili's shoulder, ensuring she'd definitely be crispy by the time Mount Paula finished venting.

"You fucking bitch."

Oh, here we go, thought Chili as she sighed. She figured the horns and leathery wings would come next, so she tried to move a stool over before she got strangled with the long forked tongue she was sure Paula hid well. "They also gave me the power to fire you, so stop talking right now and let me finish," she said as she grabbed Paula's hand so she couldn't step away from her.

"Don't give me that shit," Paula said, her voice rising to a shriek usually heard only in theaters full of tween girls watching horror movies. "You've been waiting for this since you fucked me and dumped me once the sheets got cold."

"Problem?"

The question and who was asking it made Chili hope this was the part of her nightmare where she woke up and laughed at the absurdity of this scenario actually happening. Since she wasn't that lucky, she had no choice but to answer. "We were discussing strategy. What brings you here?"

"I have dinner with my father here once a week. The food's good and you can't beat the view, but it's usually quieter." As Sam was talking, Maria got off the elevator and joined them with a large smile.

"I guess Huey isn't the only one who likes the view."

"Who gives a shit," Paula said loudly. "This isn't over, so don't make a lot of plans with Virgil. When I'm done you'll be the one taking shit from me."

"Your vocabulary hasn't expanded much, and to finish what I was going to say before your brain short-circuited, I wasn't planning to get rid of you." The way Sam stared at her made her take her own advice, and she stopped talking. "Good night to all of you."

Maria put her arm around Sam's waist as she finished her beer. It couldn't be anything intimate, since Maria was in a relationship, but it was more familiar than pure friendship. If it was, Sam had never mentioned it, and she wasn't about to ask why Maria had gone through the dance she had about asking her permission to interview Sam. Any more surprises and the greeter job at Walmart would become more enticing.

"That's it." Paula's voice was now at a level Chili was sure had dogs howling in the streets. "Run away like you always do, but I'm going to make you pay."

"Uh-huh," she said, putting money on the bar and desperately trying to think of any prayer the nuns had crammed into her head when she was in Catholic school. The fact she'd survived the demon pack of rabid penguins with their rosary beads, which were in fact the original weapons of mass-ass destruction, gave her the courage to face anything. "I paid and now I'm walking. If that or anything else tonight is in any way newsworthy—" She left the rest unsaid for Maria.

"I'm only here for the view, the company, and the steak. The next time we speak professionally we'll have a new senator. You have my word," Maria said.

"Uh-huh," she repeated as she saw Paula's hand come up, so she took a quick step to the left to avoid it. "Thank you for shopping at Wally World," she mumbled, and Sam stepped closer.

"Did you say something?" Sam asked.

"Nothing important—just talking to myself about my to-do list. Enjoy your night."

CHAPTER SIX

Sam arrived at Virgil's headquarters the next morning and helped the film crew set up for the spots they were shooting once Chili, Virgil, and Paula were done in the office. The door was closed, and so far all she'd heard was Paula's voice. Like the night before, she didn't sound thrilled.

"Somebody's not happy, huh?" the guy with the camera asked her.

"Yeah, but you guys know not to talk about all this, right?" She briefly glanced at him before she went back to staring at the door, willing it to open.

"And have Chili rip my balls off, light them on fire, and feed them to me? No worries about anybody here. We're all cool. I was just making an observation."

Almost as if by her sheer will the door opened and Paula was the first one out. She appeared angry, and she glared at Chili once she'd stomped over to the closest chair, but aside from the visible hostility, she kept quiet.

"What's going on?" Sam asked Chili, once the director took Virgil to his mark and screamed at his camera guy to get going.

"Paula got a new job, and she'd like nothing better than to stab me in the eye with a Vote-for-Virgil pin to celebrate her demotion." Chili gave the director a thumbs-up once he'd set up the first shot with Virgil in it.

"You still aren't going to tell me why she hates you so much but obviously still wants you?"

"I'm sure you've gotten that story by now, and Paula wants me as much as she wants to tattoo *Stupid* on her forehead. Never mind that it'd fit her and serve as a warning to the world at large."

"Why would I ask you if I knew that?" She was amazed at Virgil's transformation and how beautiful his wife was when she stepped in and took her place behind his stool. With his new clothes they made a very attractive couple.

"You had dinner with Maria Poplin last night, right?" Sam nodded. "Then I'm sure your date was thrilled to give you a complete report. If she didn't volunteer it, I'm sure you asked."

"Maria didn't give up any of your secrets, and she wasn't my date." Chili still wouldn't make eye contact, and it bothered her. "If it makes a difference I don't care what your history with her is. Paula's obviously a bit unhinged, so it's a good thing that history is all you share with her now."

"No, all her screws are in tight," Chili said, and laughed. "The people who fall in her web are the ones that have the problems."

"Ah, a hint," she said, and winked at Chili when she finally looked at her.

"It's more of a warning than a hint."

"No, I'm taking it as a hint." She glanced back at Paula and the scowl was still in place. "Paula's not my type."

"With smarts like that, I should be flogged for calling you unteachable."

"That can be arranged," Sam said, and Chili laughed.

❖

Two weeks went by and Sam was no closer to getting to the truth about Paula and Chili, so she went back on her promise to herself at her weekly dinner with Huey. "Daddy, do you know Paula?"

"Paula Stern who works for Virgil Emery? That Paula?"

"That's the one." She nodded to the waiter when he held the wine bottle Huey had ordered over her glass.

"I'm acquainted with her, but I don't know her well. Why, is there a problem?"

"I was just wondering about her and Chili."

He took a sip of his wine, then stared at it as if he'd find the perfect answer in the amber liquid. They had picked Ruth's Chris Steak House that night because he loved the atmosphere. They'd run into a few others in the same business who wanted to talk shop, but Huey had waved them off as they'd made their way to a semi-private table in the corner. "Before I answer your question and we start talking about Paula, let me tell you that I love Chili like part of our family."

"I know that," she said before taking a small sip of wine and almost stopping him before he said anything else. All of a sudden it wasn't important to know the story of Paula and Chili.

"Every so often Chili's got about as much willpower as the devil on Sunday. Paula was one of those temptations she should've passed up but didn't, and it was rather turbulent at the end."

"I've never known you to be a prude, Daddy."

"I'm not. It's just that for all the good qualities I want you to learn from, like her instincts when it comes to political advantage, I want you to stay the hell away from her socially." He put his hands up and held them higher when Sam started to say something. "I know exactly how old you are and that I sound like a meddling old man, but I'm right about this. Chili Alexander is bad news when it comes to women."

"And how do you know I'm into women?"

"Because I've never known you to date anyone of the

male persuasion, and you gave new meaning to sorority-sister closeness when you were at Tulane." Huey chuckled. "I don't want you to try to change anything about yourself to make the world or me happy, Sam, but I don't want you to set yourself up for a world of hurt either."

"I'll keep that in mind."

"I mean it. You're old enough to know better, but I'm your father and it's my job to save you from a cartload of trouble when I can."

"Whatever happened must've been something," she said, trying to sound dismissive of the subject.

"Crap like that got more than enough people to call me and tell me to stay the hell away from Chili when she came to me for a job." The waiter put down their oysters Rockefeller and left them to their talk after he refilled their wineglasses. "Chili, though, does a good job of selling herself, so I took a chance. My gamble paid off, and I laugh whenever I see those concerned folks who warned me about the problem child I was taking on. Every one of those bastards was waiting for me to fire her after Paula so they could pounce."

"Politics isn't for the faint of heart, for sure."

"No, but if you're good at what you do it is forgiving—Bill Clinton proved that. Sex isn't the death knell it used to be, and I think Chili learned her lesson when it comes to indiscretions biting you in the ass. She's a little more careful now, but she's still a player that isn't about to slow down, from what I see."

She rolled her wineglass between her hands and nodded. It wasn't the entire story but enough of it to reach some sound conclusions without pushing her dad for any more. "Virgil and his wife certainly love her."

"Of course they do. Chili is good at delivering on the kinds of promises she's making them. She's a master of the game, the best I've come across, really, but remember what I said. Keep your distance when it comes to anything but work."

"Not that I'm interested, and I'm not, but aren't you being a little harsh? You said she learned her lesson, so why not cut her some slack?"

The way he pressed his lips together meant he had his mind set on the subject and defiance would have consequences, and because her father was the most overprotective man she knew when it came to her, this time Chili would pay even if Sam made the first move.

"She's brilliant, but you deserve someone better, and nothing will change my mind about that." Huey picked up an oyster with his cocktail fork and held it over the plate as if she'd pinged his worry antenna. "Is there something I should know?" The way his face had paled she thought he'd be sick if she told him she was in love with Chili.

"Nothing. I was curious since Chili acts like a nervous cat whenever Paula's within ten feet of her. I figured you'd know why. Besides, I'm too busy for a social life at the moment." She laughed and pushed his fork closer to his mouth. "I hear the owner is a real bear about that."

❖

Huey ate the oyster and stayed quiet, but his mind went into overdrive. He'd seen this more than once, and he'd dubbed it the Chili fog. That Sam was smitten made his stomach turn to stone. She wasn't fooling him. This much curiosity would lead to the quest to satisfy it, and if Chili laid a hand on Sam, he'd kill her.

"Are you sure you're okay?" Sam asked when their waiter delivered the crème brûlée he'd no longer wanted to order, much less eat, but that had been the fifth time Sam had asked him the same question.

"I'm fine. Go ahead and eat before the whipped cream in those strawberries melts." Sam had changed the subject and hadn't mentioned Chili again, but she was smart enough to read his mood. Whatever else she wanted to know about Chili and whatever she was going to do with that knowledge was something she'd keep to herself. His reaction had cut him out of her loop.

Sam stared at him as he studied the bill, and she sighed. From an early age, that sigh had been her tell that something was bothering her. "You want to come over and watch a movie?" she asked.

"Not tonight, sweetheart. I'm heading home after this and going to bed. It's been a long couple of days, and I'm ready for an early night in."

"Promise me something then."

"You name it and I'll do it for you."

"It's not about me, Daddy. If you're really going home, then great, but if you're not, don't do anything you'll regret."

He laughed at how perceptive Sam had become over the years. "I try never to do that, and I'm not really sure what you're talking about."

"Come on, don't play possum with me. If you go with your heart on this one, you're going to jeopardize something you might not be able to repair. You're the greatest guy I know, but that'll only get you so far once you blow up a bridge you count on."

Sam didn't say anything else and smiled almost sadly when he kissed her cheek as he helped her into her car. Despite her lecture, he stared at his watch until she was out of the parking lot. It was still early so he decided on a drive before heading home. Chili's domain wasn't a place he visited often, and he envied the slice of peace she'd found so close to the city.

Her car was there, but it wasn't the only one in the small lot. Did he chance barging in on Chili entertaining or wait? He'd have to do what he had in mind here since he didn't want to take his insecurities into the office. His decision was easy when he saw another one of the houseboats lit up and a couple out on their deck. If Chili was entertaining, they'd carpooled.

He knocked and saw the wall of televisions on, the largest one in the center on ESPN, but he didn't see Chili sprawled as usual on the large leather couch, which was one of the first things she'd bought when she'd started working for him. If the thing could talk he was sure it'd have a bestseller on its hands.

"Hey, boss," Chili said, startling him into slamming against her door. Chili was covered in sweat, and goose bumps were starting to rise on her arms because of the cold night air. "Something wrong?"

"Can I bother you for a scotch?"

Chili ushered him in and kicked off her running shoes before she poured the drink he'd asked for. She came back with a sports drink and waved for him to sit. "Besides my liquor, what else can I do for you? Not that I'm not happy to see you, but home visits aren't your style unless you've got something on your mind."

"First, promise me you aren't going to get pissed and throw me into that freezing water outside when you hear what I have to say." He wet his lips with the scotch.

"I can narrow the reason for that request down to two people," Chili said as she sat across from Huey on her large coffee table. Huey acted like a shy schoolboy who had to tattle on his best friends only when he had to participate in distasteful conversations centered around sexual things that weren't his business. "Is it Sam or Paula?"

"Both, actually." He wet his lips again, but the level in the glass didn't go down, so she took the opportunity to finish hers. "Sam and I had dinner tonight and she was full of questions about Paula."

"I bet." She laughed and thought of a quote she'd read once but couldn't remember who'd said it. It was something about no matter how rich you became you could never buy back your past. Your mistakes were yours forever, and no matter how much distance and time you put between them and the present, they'd always be there to suck the life out of you when you least expected it. "Did she enjoy the gossip she's been after since she first met Paula?"

"Come on. I'm not that much of an old hen. I told her Paula was a mistake and to let it go. Considering she said you can't stand the sight of her, I doubt it's one you're apt to repeat."

When he wet his lips again she sighed. "Either drink the damn thing or let me get you some lip balm."

"All right. I don't really want to have this conversation, but I don't want to not have it. You know how important Sam is to me."

"Got it. Paws off Sam and remember my place. Consider it done, but you were right. We didn't need to have this talk. For one, Sam tolerates me but isn't what I consider a friend."

"She wouldn't have asked if she doesn't like you. That's how Sam is."

"I'll take your word for it, but from what I see, she'll be a great successor when you're ready to retire since she knows how to keep her distance. Second, I know better. I'm an idiot when it comes to women but I'm not a predator, and I'm also the hired help." She crushed the plastic bottle and took a couple of deep breaths because she didn't blame Huey for this. The haunting that was Paula was back and rattling chains so loud no one, especially Chili, could ignore them.

"If I even thought that…well, you know the rest. I care a great deal for you, Chili, but I want Sam to have a fresh start. Hell, that doesn't sound good either." He did drain the glass after his stumbling explanations. "You aren't going to quit on me, are you?"

"For being an asshole but a good dad?" He laughed since she hadn't said it with any malice, but she couldn't bring herself to join him. "I'm not that vindictive, so you're stuck with me. With any luck I'll dance at Sam's wedding when she marries some guy with a name like Bradford." They'd often joked about some of the society guys who were born into money and given those old family names, but whose heads were often empty and who lacked ambition. All they could be grateful for was that one of their ancestors had the drive to make the fortune all the family lived off forever. She and Huey also joked that all the Bradfords of the world had won the genetic lottery, but because of them future generations would be screwed.

"Fuck you too," Huey said as he stood and held his hand out. "Hopefully you'll wait until I'm dead before you go, so don't go breaking an old man's heart."

"Cut the shit, Huey. What else is on your mind? Or did whatever you ate upset your stomach so much it made you sound like a melancholy old matron."

"There was one other thing," he said as he jammed his hands into his pants pockets. "Someone told me you had breakfast up at the capital recently. Word is you had a new job on the menu."

"You're the worst gossip in the world, Huey, and you're old enough to know you shouldn't believe everything you hear."

"Who was it?"

"Rooster called and I answered. I owe him as much as I owe you, so it was me doing him a favor to return the million he's done for me. If you want to know everything we talked about, he's got his heart set on DC and he did offer me a job, like he does every time I see him. Hell, he even does it when you're in the room, and my answer's always the same." She took his hand and made him sit down again. "Everything else okay? Or did you come over here to beat up on me to make yourself feel better?"

"Nothing, except my job with Sam is almost done. Now that she's on her own I don't know what I'll do with myself. Then every time I turn around someone's trying to steal you away."

"Take up knitting. With practice you can corner the market on penis cozies. It'll keep you busy until Bradford and Sam give you grandchildren. Then you can plan and run their campaign for the presidency, or you can add more money to their trust fund."

"I come here, insult you more than once, and end up getting comforted by you. How the hell does that always happen?"

"Go home and figure it out, and once you're in bed, sleep peacefully knowing Sam's going to be okay." She pulled him up this time and walked him to the door. "If you don't believe that, then go to sleep thinking about what I'm going to do to you, like putting ipecac in that special-reserve scotch you love so much."

"That sounds more like you," Huey said as he waved over his shoulder when he was on her gangplank. "Thanks for not giving me a black eye I'd have to explain tomorrow."

"Don't thank me yet. You never know what kind of mood I'll be in tomorrow, and speaking of tomorrow, don't take a lot of calls." He stopped and faced her. "Every once in a while I love gossip myself, and I know for sure this time it's got merit, so we don't want anyone to get the idea any of it came from our shop."

"Did it?"

"Nothing like this will ever come from us, but it doesn't mean we can't ride the wave that's going to come when a piece of shit this big falls in the toilet bowl."

"Your next career should be in speech writing. You have such an eloquent way of putting things."

"Quit while you're ahead and stay away from the phone. And remember I still love you."

Chili stripped her running clothes off as soon as Huey left and stepped into the shower. When she got under the strong hot spray a thought occurred to her. Why should Huey worry about her when it came to Sam? Then the image of Maria with her arm around Sam's waist came to her. In a way she'd watched Sam grow up, but she hadn't spent any time really concentrating on Huey's precious little girl except when she'd needed help with her homework once she'd gotten to Tulane.

But once Sam had gone to Tulane and come out of her shell a little, Chili had every so often really taken notice. She wouldn't go as far as what Dale had said about a crush, but Sam was a classic beauty, and when she was excited about something she had a way of pulling people in with her laugh and enthusiasm. When Sam smiled, Chili became curious as to who Sam would end up with. Whoever it was, she figured they'd be addicted to Sam's laugh for the rest of their lives.

"Seems I've been missing out."

CHAPTER SEVEN

For the next few weeks Chili sent Sam out with Virgil and Candy as they campaigned at the locations Chili knew would be full of sure voters for a campaign that would have a historically low turnout. The Emery campaign was finishing its rounds at the local VFW and retirement homes in Virgil's district, and Chili knew it would be brutal if the people they met with were for the other guy. Age lowered the usual filter people had when it came to saying exactly what was on their minds.

Brutal or not, all the activity had kept Sam away from her until she figured out how to handle Huey's reprimand or, more accurately, his shot across her bow for something she really hadn't planned to do. After some thought and time, she was still angry, but it wasn't fair to take it out on Sam.

She drove to the retirement home on Virgil's schedule for the day, and from the laughter coming from the cafeteria she was sure Virgil was a born campaigner. He had a large group of people in wheelchairs around him, and he spoke with his usual passion with his tie slightly undone and his sleeves rolled up. Chili's staff had stopped and bought cupcakes iced with Christmas colors, and she was happy to see everyone in the audience enjoying the treats.

"You with Roosevelt over there?" the old man coming in with the help of a walker asked.

"Yes, sir, can I get you a cupcake?" She pulled a chair out for him when he stopped next to her.

"You think I'm going to sell my vote for a cupcake with a Christmas tree on it?"

"No, but if I can't talk you into eating one, will you tell me what you think?"

"Been listening for an hour before my weak pisser couldn't hold out. Sounds honest enough, but he's as slick as a used-car salesman." The old guy sat down and looked her in the eye, but judging by the way he had his head cocked he still seemed to be listening to Virgil. Despite his initial rejection he took one of the treats off the tray she'd brought him from the table.

"Would you vote for him?" Most everyone on her staff, Sam now probably included, thought these outings were a waste of time. Their polling techniques were so good, talking to individual voters for the simple exercise of conversation didn't really seem necessary, but sometimes you found that big nugget of gold in the over-mined riverbed.

"Would you?" the man shot back.

"I vote in every election I'm eligible for, no matter what, and if I could vote for Mr. Emery, I would."

"Guy's paying you to say that, so that's a shocker."

She laughed at the guy's straightforwardness. "You don't have to believe me, but when you take Virgil's background into account, I mean really look at where he started and what he's made of himself, I can't help but respect him. I won't vote for someone I don't trust or respect, no matter how much money they throw at me. With Virgil, I'd know what I'm getting."

"What's that, a good jalopy with four bald tires?"

"Not a lot of polish, but a sound businessman who knows how to get things done. In my experience, really nice guys who tell you what you want to hear only work hard to get themselves reelected." Sam must've heard her laugh and was walking toward them. "Why won't you vote for him?"

"Didn't say that. Who's your friend?" he asked when Sam sat next to her.

"This is Sam and she'd vote for Virgil too, if you were wondering." She smiled at Sam and lost it when she turned back to their new friend. "One more question, then I'll let you go give Virgil hell. What would you tell our guy to do differently if you were in charge?"

"How do you know I can answer that?"

"Call it a hunch."

"If what you say is true about his growing up, get his mama out talking about him. Is she still kicking?"

"Mrs. Emery is now living a comfortable life because of Virgil." Virgil's mother was that, but she also looked like someone who thought the more bling and rhinestones on her clothes, the better. Considering Virgil's district, Chili had kept her under wraps.

"Then take her out of mothballs and let her brag a bit about her son. A boy who loves and takes care of his mama sounds a hell of lot better than a used-car salesman."

"Mr. Emery actually sells luxury Japanese cars," Sam said, and the old man gave her an amused look.

"Yeah, that'll help."

"What's your name and who'd you work for?" Chili asked, thinking she and Sam were being tweaked.

"Bob Beson at your service, and before my family locked me up in here I spent some time with Governor Delwood."

"Before or after his federal indictment and subsequent prosecution?" Sam asked, and Chili laughed again. "You'll be happy to know he's got his own chapter in the Louisiana Political History course I took at Tulane."

"Did all that education you got also tell you he was the only guy ever elected four times to that office, and the best damn campaigner on the stump since the Longs? My job was a sight easier with Delwood than you'll have with this hillbilly with the new tie."

"Thanks, Bob," Chili said, as she slapped his shoulder. "You can stop teasing the animals now, but that mom spot is a good idea."

"If it makes you feel any better, your opponent was here last week, and all he talked about were your big guns and inexperience. The old biddies didn't take to him as much as Virgil and the pretty harem serving treats he brought with him," he said, looking at Sam.

"We always hire for brains, but pretty is certainly a bonus," she said, and Sam's expression was one of amused tolerance. "I just can't admit that or I'd face being sued for harassment."

"My family might've dumped me the first chance they got so I can't work anymore, but at least I'm not dealing with all that shit you have to put up with. The workplace was a hell of a lot more entertaining when you could call a girl 'honey,' and she didn't have a conniption over it while her friends immediately formed a protest line outside the office."

"We try to keep that to a minimum at our place," Chili said, and laughed for one of the first times since Huey had come to her house.

"You do realize she's a woman, right?" Sam asked Bob.

"Honey, you do realize who your boss is, right? Delwood won so much because the ladies loved him, but he didn't get to break that four-time record when he butted heads with poll-vaulter Chili Alexander. Talk about someone who had every lady in the room trying to get her opinion on something. At least that's what they call it these days." Bob laughed like he'd said something brilliantly clever, but Chili tried to keep a straight face.

"Yes, I know who my boss is, but I'm one of those women who don't see the charm in being called sweetheart."

"Who the heck called you sweetheart? I called you honey. It's a term of endearment, not a proposition." Bob stood and positioned himself at the center of his walker. "Come back if you need any more advice or if you need a date to anything and the big girl there won't take you. Let's see what else the car salesman has in his arsenal."

"Did you know who he was?" Sam asked as Bob limped away.

"Why do you always think I'm setting you up for something?" Chili waved any response off from Sam and tried to tamp down the irritation in her voice. Why Huey would worry that Sam was in any way interested in her made her head spin. Hell, if she made a pass at her, Sam was liable to stab her through the heart with the Montblanc pen she loved to carry around. "Actually, that was a surprise, but it goes to show that places like this are full of talent, even if they're forgotten."

"Yeah, I feel like that these days," Sam said as she sat back and crossed her legs. "Did you come by to check up on me, or to tell me you don't really need me around? Or better yet, you're here for me to get you some coffee and call me sweetheart."

"I believe Bob said it was honey, but it's none of those things." The news she'd been waiting on to kick off Rooster's campaign had been delayed since the fact-checkers were still hard at work making sure everything they were going to make public was true.

She'd called in a few favors and gotten the faith-based gathering to push back their meeting. When the story broke she wanted it fresh on their minds, not months later when the spin had cooled the shock factor. Rooster had done well with the chamber of commerce and the oilmen, but that had been a given. It was time to make some inroads in demographics that won elections.

"I thought you might want to go with me tomorrow. I'm Senator Roberts's guest at the preacher luncheon in Alexandria."

Sam stared at her like she usually did, and as usual she felt dissected. "Are you sure? Lately I get the impression you're done with me, like Bob's family is with him." Sam smiled and shrugged. "I thought you might think I'm unteachable."

"That's truer of me than you, but I try to learn something new every day to balance out my ignorance."

"I'm not sure what that means, but I'd love to come. Do you mind finishing up here? I've got an appointment I couldn't reschedule and was about to call Beth to fill in for me."

"Go ahead, and I'll meet you at the office at eight. We're taking Rooster's plane from Lakefront to save us the long drive."

Sam nodded and shouldered her bag as if she couldn't get out of there fast enough. "See you then."

"I thought the semi-silent treatment would be better than the constant questions about Paula," Chili said softly as Sam practically ran from the room. The only time she saw Sam now was at their meetings at the office, and when she'd stopped trying to spend time with her, Sam seemed to have gotten the message and barely talked to her anymore.

For someone who loved her job, it'd become a never-ending root canal lately, and the numbing shots were starting to wear off. She scrubbed her face with her hands and tried her best to pay attention to Virgil. "It's not good to be wrong this much."

❖

"What in the hell did you tell Chili?" Sam asked her father after slamming her way into his office. "Don't try to deny it either."

"Nothing she should've shared with you."

His answer was confirmation enough. The only other time she'd been this humiliated, her dance teacher was in tears after Huey hadn't cared for her comments on her ballet moves. It wasn't surprising that tutus still made her twitchy. "Spill it, Daddy."

"What, so you can compare our stories?"

"No, I want to know why she acts like I'm a highly contagious leper. All that happened after the night we had dinner and you rushed the meal to run off somewhere." Sam pointed at him and tried not to scream. "I ask a few lousy questions about some old flame, and you talked to her about me? What did you tell her? And I mean word for word so I can fix what you did."

"That's nonsense...come on, honey. You're imagining things. You've been busy with Virgil's campaign, but that's not the only thing going on. Chili's been preoccupied with a couple of other races that'll be important for us to be involved in. She doesn't have time to hover over you, no matter if I think the whole world should."

"Don't call me honey ever again, and that's all you're going to say? You know I'm going to find out, so why not admit to it now?" Her father never appeared rattled, no matter what, but he couldn't look her in the eye, so he was totally guilty.

"Nothing to admit to, so relax."

"Okay," she said, and sighed hard enough to not be overly dramatic. "I thought you had enough faith in me to make my way here. It's disappointing to know that's not true."

Huey's facade finally cracked a little when he stood and pressed his hands together. "You'll be successful with or without Chili Alexander."

"If you don't trust me to learn from the person you think has better instincts than you do, I'll never get the opportunity to find that out." She left after she said that, sensing that it was better to keep the conversation unfinished. He was standing in the doorway of his office when the elevator doors closed, but she ignored his raised hand.

"Do you think my father would've threatened Chili into

staying away from me?" she asked Maria when she answered her phone.

"Yes, and probably more than once, but before you go off the deep end, let me ask you something. Do you think you're a little obsessed with Chili?"

"No, but I want to get to know her. Hell, I've heard about her from everyone we have in common, but no one wants to let me make up my own mind about her." She sighed again and fell against the back of the elevator wall. "I'm not a simpleton who needs the world at large to keep her out of trouble."

"That's why I haven't answered all your questions, buddy. I try to get Chili on air whenever I can because she's the whole package, but not without a few flaws. Are the flaws big enough to stay the hell away from her? Hell, no. I like her enough that if I didn't have Danielle waiting at home, I would've made a play for her by now."

"That seems to be my father's biggest fear, and whatever he told her made Chili back down so fast she left a chill in the air."

"Do you think she was interested?"

"Any way I answer that makes me look pathetic."

"Sam, come on, be honest. Do you like her?" Maria asked compassionately.

"She barely talks to me anymore so I can't really answer that. Even though we've known each other for years, I can't answer that truthfully since you know me better than to think I'd be interested in someone simply because she's good-looking." She unlocked her car and hoped she wouldn't hit a lot of traffic on the way home.

"Incredibly good-looking, you mean?" Maria said, and laughed.

"Don't make fun of me."

"Okay, sorry. If you want my advice, play the same game she is right now, and that'll get her interested more than anything.

You know the old sayings about distance and fondness. If this is something you want, then go for it no matter what Huey or anyone else thinks. All I want is for you to be happy."

Sam's phone signaled another call coming in. "Can you hold up a minute? It's Chili." She took a deep breath and answered. "Hey, you need something?"

"Think Maria would want to come with us tomorrow?"

"You want me to call her?" This was a strange request, considering Chili knew Maria well and could've done it herself.

"I'll do it if you don't have time, but I figured you two are close."

Sam detected plenty of innuendo in that statement, but now wasn't the time to call Chili on it. "Sure, I'll be glad to. Any particular reason you want her along? You don't give me the impression you like any media around you unless there's something in it for a client."

"And you say you're unteachable," Chili said, and laughed. "If it helps convince her, tell her there's something in it for her, and I'll be happy to do another interview whenever she likes. I'll owe her one."

"Careful. She'll definitely take you up on that."

"I'm counting on it."

"Okay." She stretched out the word. "Hopefully you'll trust me enough to eventually tell me what's going on."

"Sometimes surprises aren't such bad things, Sam, and I do trust you. Call me back if Maria needs convincing."

"How's the dynamic Chili?" Maria asked when she came back on the line.

"She wants you to come to Alexandria with Senator Roberts tomorrow. How about it?"

"Did she say why?"

"She said there's something in it for you as well as another interview with her whenever you want."

"Now that's an interesting proposition coming from Chili Alexander. I'm in," Maria said, and hung up as fast as Chili had. "Let's hope eventually I'll be in too."

❖

Their flight was uneventful, and everyone on the plane pretty much spent the forty-five-minute trip with either their eyes closed or glued to a laptop. Maria looked between Sam and Chili but didn't say anything to break the peace that lasted until they landed.

"Do I get a hint any time soon?" Maria asked Chili when Chili pointed to the second car waiting in the hangar they'd pulled into. "Or are you busy putting up big hand-grenade cutouts on Virgil's headquarters, and you wanted us out of town so we couldn't cover it?"

"You're hilarious, and I was thinking more like some big elephants waving little Confederate flags, but Virgil shot me down." Chili opened the back door and waved Maria, her cameraman, and Sam into the backseat. "Believe me, by day's end I'll be your new best friend. Hell, you might even get me something nice for Christmas and my birthday."

"That's a tall order, since I only have a week to shop."

They arrived at the large auditorium that reminded Chili of her high school PE days, but so far everyone had been very cordial. "They seem nice enough," Rooster said, as if reading her mind.

"They sure are, but believe me, right now they'd rather invite Satan over for Christmas dinner than vote for you. Remember what I've told you about thirty times now. Read that speech word for word, and no matter what happens, don't get rattled."

"I trust you with my life, Chili, but what the shit does that mean?"

"Like George Bush promised us at the beginning of his presidency, shock and awe is what will happen here today, and these guys will see the light, as it were." She moved closer to him and put her hand on his shoulder. "If you really want this, today's the day to take it away from the asshole who has that office now."

The lunch started, and Sam looked at her and raised her eyebrows when they were asked to stand for a prayer before the food was served and Chili glanced at her phone while the older man with a thick north Louisiana accent prayed for their salvation before the rubber chicken and bad potatoes were served. The text Chili had gotten simply said "takeoff." She put her hand in Chili's collar and pulled her head down so she could whisper in her ear. "Start praying before one of these zealots throws us out of here."

The soft breath along with the incredible dress Sam had on made Chili wish they had a few seats between them. All she could do was nod and say amen along with the large congregation. When the preacher finished, there was definitely no sense of separation of church and state here, and they didn't pretend to care that the forefathers had insisted on that concept for the government they'd formed.

"So, Senator Roberts, are you looking forward to retirement?" Reverend Buford Jones, the president of the North Louisiana Baptist Association, asked with what Chili thought was an insincere smile. "Surely you're not thinking of becoming a daddy again?" Buford laughed, and the two other preachers at their table joined in with a bit too much gusto.

The way Rooster glared at her, she could tell the piece of chicken he'd put in his mouth had turned to dust. Events like this were exercises in patience, because no matter how much you wanted to either punch someone or tell them to fuck off, you couldn't. You had to take every insult with a smile and move on. She smiled and slightly shook her head to keep Rooster calm.

Someone's phone dinged close to them, and Chili almost

spit out her sweetened tea when she heard the first wave of "holy hells." She put her hand on Sam's forearm when she reached in her purse for her phone and shook her head. The only person close to them she cared about checking the breaking news was Maria, and from her expression, Chili had put her in the perfect location to cover this story.

"What in tar hill is going on?" Buford asked as the whole room seemed to forget about the bad food and sickeningly sweet tea and the murmurs grew louder.

"Is there a television in here?" Chili asked, trying to help things along.

Buford pointed to the man closest to him, and he went to the set near the stage. The local station had cut away to their national affiliates, and the pretty boy reporting the news couldn't talk fast enough as the perp-walk footage played over and over. Usually a prostitution-ring roundup wasn't national news, but then again, usually two of the men in handcuffs weren't senators.

Chili had known this was coming, but this was even better than she could've hoped for. She was anticipating only the mention of the asshole Billy Fudge's name as a client of the DC ring, but seeing him in his undershirt handcuffed to a beautiful but skimpily dressed woman trying to shield his face from the camera was manna from heaven. He was trying to hide as they brought the twenty or so men and their paid dates into the police station, but there was no mistaking him and that usually primped hair that was now going in all directions.

"This has to be a mistake," Buford said as he clutched his chest. "Senator Fudge is a personal friend and a man of God."

"Seems he's also a personal friend of the DC Madame Roxie Little and her working girls," Chili said, as she smiled in Sam's direction. She stayed quiet and let the anchor finish the story, spouting the scoop they'd had for days. Fudge wasn't just literally caught with his pants down; he'd been Roxie's client for over ten years and had made some of his dates from the hallowed floor of the United States Senate. She couldn't have written a better scenario for the kickoff of Rooster's Senate campaign than if she'd found a magic lamp and the genie inside had granted her three wishes.

"I hope this doesn't mean you're not interested in talking to us today," Buford said to Rooster, the color in his face going paler by the second.

"I'm sure it won't be as exciting as all this commotion, but I'd love to," Rooster said, and patted the pocket where Chili's speech was carefully folded.

It was a blend of his positions, his vision for the future, and a smidgeon of scripture that would leave a favorable impact with the audience. Any more and it would've come across as insincere, even though Rooster was himself a man of God, as Buford had described Senator Fudge. The right had hijacked the Lord, gun control, and defense as their issues, and any Democrat trying to impinge on those holy grails was usually met with disdain, but Chili had done her best to knock some of those beliefs to the curb with the speech she'd personally written, something she rarely did anymore.

"How in the hell did you know about this?" Sam asked when she followed Chili out of the room to the hallway that led to the bathrooms. "There's no way you're this lucky if Rooster really does want to run."

"He does want to run, and he needs a little more than a fourth of the voters from here to the Arkansas border to win. That's all you have to know right now. It's not like I set old Billy up with the stacked blonde he's had a standing appointment with for years." She pointed to the door so Sam would go back in. "Later on, if you want, you can ask questions, but right now we want all the talk to be about the senator with the paid girlfriends and not about anyone who came with Rooster."

Sam walked away, giving her a little privacy for the call she had to make. "Thank you," she said, when Sophie Grossman answered.

"I'm sure I owe you a few more favors, but are we close to getting even?"

"You don't owe me anything, Sophie." The applause from the auditorium was more enthusiastic than she thought it would be, despite the story about Fudge, which was a good sign. A love affair as long as these guys had had with Fudge didn't die in a day, but she wanted Rooster to make an impact. Fudge would win some of them back with Bible references and heartfelt apologies soon enough, but all Rooster needed was for some of them to doubt his word. "I told you that a long time ago, and I meant it. Thanks, though. If today had been a movie set, I couldn't have written a better script."

"No matter what, you never heard about this from me. To pay me back, beat this prick and replace him with Rooster. I think it'll be a night-and-day difference, and it'll be a hell of lot better covering him in the Senate. At least Rooster doesn't make me feel like I need a shower when I'm done interviewing him."

Sophie had started as the traffic girl at the NBC affiliate in New Orleans and had been promoted to the desk a year later. It took less than five years after that for the national folks to notice and steal her away. Before that had happened, Chili and Sophie had a really good time together, but Sophie had wanted the whole package, including a ring and everything that came with it. She'd run so fast after Sophie made that point clear, that Sophie's decision to move on had been easy for her.

But before Sophie had moved she'd done a story and hadn't had every fact verified, and the consequences had almost cost her everything. Chili had called in almost every chip she was owed, but she'd killed the fallout, and Sophie had been trying to pay back the favor ever since.

"You're doing good up there, so don't take any more chances

like this. Granted, this really helped, but I don't want any of this to come back and bite you if anyone ties this to you."

"Unless you're planning to tell on me, don't worry about it." Sophie sounded like she was in the car, and Chili hoped she was alone. "Have you made any progress in becoming an adult?"

"Just because you're engaged doesn't mean the rest of the world has to be in love. I do appreciate that you still worry about that."

"You're still important to me, and as hard as your cowardice was on my heart, it's the best thing that ever happened to me. I might be down there in a month or less, so don't think about turning me down for dinner, and I want you to take me some place expensive. Start saving up. We'll discuss your love life over the best seafood you can find, and I'll tell you how blissfully happy I am."

"You got it, so stay out of trouble until then."

Sam was waiting for her in the doorway, and she got back in time to see Rooster working the room with Carla at his side. These yahoos needed to remember that Rooster would never stray from the woman at his side.

"Hopefully if you think of continuing your career, Senator Roberts, you'll come up this way again. We'd be interested in helping you put together a platform we'd all be happy with," Buford said as he shook Rooster's hand.

"I'll hold you to that, but I still have some things to consider before I make my final decision," Rooster said, and Buford's entourage leaned in, listening. "I want to make sure my wife is okay with the idea, and I'd like to avoid a negative campaign. That's not my style."

"Ma'am," Buford said, taking Carla's hand, "your husband still has a lot to offer this state, so I hope you steer him in the right direction."

Sam rolled her eyes, but only so Chili could see. "Want to grab a drink to celebrate?" Sam asked.

"I'll take a rain check, if you don't mind. After this I'm going to be busy for the next few weeks seeing how this shakes out."

"Let me know if you need me to do anything."

"You can start by not telling Paula that Rooster's running," she said, and laughed.

❖

"She asked you out and you turned her down?" Dale asked as he browned onions in Chili's kitchen.

"Did you forget the part of the story I told you where her father, my boss, came over here and threatened me if I look at his daughter for more than ten seconds?" She sat in her den and, for once, really enjoyed watching the news.

Fudge had made every major network, so it didn't matter which one she watched. They all showed the same shot of him handcuffed to his date, his hair mussed, and wearing an expression of total disbelief that this was happening to him. She had to give it to Fudge; he had good taste in women, even if he was paying for it. This was so good, though, she was thinking of having that video clip put on a loop and sending it out as her Christmas greeting.

"You've missed having dinner with me two weeks in a row, so fill me in on what's happening besides Huey's temporary foray into insanity."

"He's not crazy, Dale," she said, finally getting up and joining him in the kitchen. "He's worried about his daughter, and I don't have a defense about what a jerk I've been in the past when I have to see Paula practically every day. Talk about a reminder about all the mistakes I've made."

"It's not like you had three kids and a wife at home while you were with Paula. You were a single adult lured to the dark side by perky tits and a great ass. That could happen to anyone. Don't you remember that Michael Douglas movie?" He added chicken to the pot next and stirred it with a flick of his wrist. "Hell, you should be glad you didn't have a pet rabbit when that crazy bitch didn't take no too well."

"You're a riot, and you should be glad you're cooking me dinner. I'd hate to stab you before you're done."

"You love my cooking too much to harm me bad enough to put me out of commission." He added a few more spices before plating everything and handing her some dishes to take to the table. It was raining too hard to eat outside.

"Did you get a chance to pick up our anniversary gift for Mom and Dad?" They'd decided a trip to Aruba would be a good way for their parents to celebrate their second honeymoon.

"Yes, along with all the catering. Are you bringing a date?"

"Are you?" she asked guiltily, since she hadn't asked Dale too much about what was happening in his life lately. She really needed to work on that before Dale finally got tired of her ignoring him and gave up on her.

"I'm thinking about inviting one of the waitresses just so I don't have to hear about how I'm going to grow old alone and regret not giving my mother grandchildren."

"Good plan. I'd bring Beth or someone from the office, but Mama would see through that the second I arrived. It's too bad Sophie won't be here till after the party. That one she might buy, until she got a look at her left ring finger, since I'm sure the producer she hooked up with must've sprung for a large stone with an equally stunning setting."

"Sophie was nice and had the spunkiest personality I've ever seen in a woman, but don't cry too hard over letting her go." She stopped eating after Dale said that. "What?" he said, shrugging. "You had a good time, and I'm sure she did, but there was never going to be anything besides that. She wasn't the one who stole your heart. That hasn't happened, from what I've seen."

"I wish I knew me as well as you seem to." Maybe they should start eating in the den so she could lie down while they talked. With enough time and ingredients, perhaps Dale could eventually fix her.

"I not only know you, but I love you, so don't forget that."

"I love you too, even if you always cancel out my vote," she said, and laughed. Dale had a way of easing her mind more than anyone else. "Maybe I should call Billy Fudge and ask where I can rent a nice girl to bring as my date."

Chapter Eight

A few days after the holidays Chili set up a few events for Virgil to get the voters interested in the campaign again. "Will you really work to fix the coast, Mr. Virgil," the young girl who'd come with some interested adult to Virgil's town hall meeting asked with such earnestness Chili considered putting her in a commercial spot. She'd always thought kids like this would get them out of the jam their parents and grandparents had put them in.

"I pinkie swear," Virgil said, holding out his little finger as he winked at the woman behind the girl.

They walked out at a leisurely pace so Virgil could shake hands and talk to whoever seemed interested in his view of the world. Chili usually left these things up to her staff, but the event was taking place near her brother's restaurant, and she was interested in seeing how well Virgil had studied. Compared to the man she'd first met, he was a completely different person and his poll numbers were nothing short of a miracle, but still not good enough to pass his opponent.

"How was that?" Virgil asked when they stepped into a small room near the space they'd rented for the event.

"Spectacular, but remember to stay on point and not run off to topics you'll have no control over in the Louisiana State Senate," she said, and Sam smiled.

"I couldn't just ignore that lady when she asked about abortion and what my stance on it was."

"Sam will review the standard answer that keeps you firmly in the middle of that debate. Usually I'd tell you to go with your belief, if you were only running in your neighborhood, but you're not. Right now you're smack in the middle of pro-life and pro-choice land, so a definitive answer that won't mean anything isn't a smart move on your part."

"I know that the Louisiana State Senate doesn't change or make federal laws."

"Damn right, and answering questions or getting into a debate about it will only alienate voters for no good reason."

"That woman was at our opponent's town hall last week," Sam said as she pulled her hair out of the ponytail she'd quickly fashioned once Virgil had starting answering questions.

"Did she ask that question then?" Chili asked.

"Nope, but she did tell him she loved his stance on gun control or, more accurately, his belief that everyone should be armed to the teeth."

"Find out when he's having another meeting, Beth, and have someone we trust go and ask the same question," Chili said as Beth took notes. "Only whoever it is, tell them to push until he gives an answer."

"You want film if we can get it?" Beth asked.

"It's a small market, but it might be worth it if you can pull it off."

"Film?" Virgil and Sam asked together.

"The woman today isn't going to vote for you, Virgil, but she did want to convince the other folks who came today into voting for her candidate. If you'd answered her, believe me, your answer would've lived on when they put it in a spot, painting you as the evil the other side of this issue always fears. When you didn't really answer, she didn't get what she came for, but since your opponent wants to play that game, we'll play too, only I like to play to win."

"That dirty son of a bitch," Virgil said. "People really do that?"

"Sometimes politics is nothing more than a game of king of the hill. You push, kick, and do whatever it takes to win and be the last guy standing, so yes, people really do that and more. I just thought they wouldn't stoop that low for this race, but we have to be ready."

"I trust you to take care of it," Virgil said, and held his hand out to Candy. "If that's all here, we've got a group of volunteers ready to walk that neighborhood on the parish line and hand out brochures."

"Have fun and beware of dogs." Chili held her hand up and pointed to the scar under her wrist. "Trust me on that too," she said, and laughed.

They all walked out together and waved to Virgil and Candy as they drove off with Beth in the backseat, after she'd volunteered to go as well. "Sorry you had to work on Saturday, but you still have time to go do something fun," Chili said to Sam.

"Do you have plans?" Sam shielded her eyes from the sun and gazed up at her. "Maybe I can cash in the drink you owe me."

"I'd love to, but today is my parents' anniversary, so my brother and I are having a party for them." The way Sam stood there after her answer made her think it would be rude not to invite her. In a way it could be the olive branch to put Sam at ease around her, since she surely wouldn't be interested. "You weren't working with us yet when the invitations went out, but if you'd like to go—"

"Sure," Sam said before she could give her an out. "You want to go in one car? And should I stop and get something?"

"Leave your car and I'll bring you back later, and all they really want is for people to have fun, so you're fine." She walked to the car thinking she'd walked right into that one, and it was too late to say she was joking.

"Do you really want me to go?" Sam asked, as if her thoughts were visible in a big cartoon bubble over her head. "If you have a date I don't want to intrude."

"You don't mind swinging by to pick up Paula?" She laughed hard at Sam's expression. "Not buying that, huh? Don't worry. I'm dateless, so maybe I asked to keep up my reputation. Can't have my cousins making fun of me for coming alone."

"I doubt anyone in your family laughs at you," Sam said as she sat and swung her legs in together. Chili watched, wondering how she'd make the move in the short skirt. "Do your cousins know what a rock star you are?"

"They vaguely remember my existence when they get a speeding ticket. Since I know a lot of people, they think they deserve a free pass and don't understand when I turn them down. The politics bug infected only me, so they're not interested too much in what I do."

"Do you want to eat before we go?" Sam asked when she stopped at the valet stand outside Dale Christian's Restaurant. They'd pooled their money to start the restaurant, so Dale thought it should be named after both of them, but she'd forced Dale to put his name first since he'd be the one slaving in the kitchen. "Party food not your thing?"

"You might not remember the night we came here with your father after the last representative's race, but this is my brother's place, so we got a good deal on the room and catering." She hurried around and gave Sam a hand out of the car. "Dale's a genius in the kitchen, but if you thought his stuff wasn't memorable, don't tell him. He's sensitive that way."

"He is a genius, and I've recommended this place more than once to my friends. Sorry the name didn't jump out at me. The last time I was here was with you."

The party room was way too small for the number of people they'd invited, so Dale had closed the entire place to accommodate the vast number of friends and family who'd showed up to wish their parents another thirty-eight of happiness. When they entered, the music was loud and a crowd covered the makeshift dance floor by the bar. Whoever wasn't dancing was engrossed in what looked like passionate conversations, but the noise level was too high to hear what was so important.

Dale spotted them and waved her over to the tables topped with serving dishes and plates. He smiled when she took Sam's hand and guided her through the crowd, stopping to say hello and thanks whenever someone stopped her. A couple of aunts were curious about Sam, so Chili kept moving before any of them offered an opinion or advice.

"You look fantastic, Sam," Dale said as he took Sam's hand when she dropped it. "Glad you could make it."

"Thanks, and thanks for the compliment. Maybe you could teach this one," Sam pointed to Chili, "that being nice isn't a crime."

"She's slow on the uptake, but if you show a little patience and don't make any sudden big moves you'll have her eating out of your hand like a skittish wild animal." Chili widened her eyes at Dale in warning. "Have one of the girls fix you a plate, and we'll sit and eat and I'll give you some pointers. I reserved a table for us."

"Don't start," Chili said, when Sam walked away. "I invited her as a courtesy and she accepted. I was shocked to hell, but that's all this is."

"And she usually needs assistance across a room when it's more than a few feet?"

"You should take up comedy, and if you try to be cute when she gets back I'm going to stick your head in the dip."

"I made the kind with shrimp that you like, so be nice to

me." He laughed as Sam came back with two plates and handed one to Chili. "That's us over there." Dale pointed to a small table with a reserved card on it. "What would you like to drink, Sam?"

"White wine or whatever, I'm not picky." Sam unfurled her napkin and glanced around the room once Dale ran off to get their drinks. "Which couple are your parents? I remember Dale, but I've never met them."

They were dancing to a slow song and moved in a way only people who've spent a lifetime together do. As a child Chili had always loved to watch her parents dance, since they seemed so happy moving to the music. They were the only people who'd been together as long as they had who were not only still madly in love with each other, but they also actually liked each other.

"There they are." She waved when her mom saw her and blew her a kiss.

"They sure look happy."

"It's no act, and they're disgustingly sappy at times, but that's part of their charm." She tried one of the selections Sam had made as she watched her parents stay on the dance floor when the tempo changed.

"My dad talks about dancing with my mom sometimes when he's feeling nostalgic, but that doesn't happen often," Sam said, sounding wistful. "At least not as often as I'd like since I'd love hearing about her every so often. He says the next time he'll voluntarily dance is at my wedding."

"Huey's a good guy, and your mom, from what I've heard of her, sounded like a good match for him. I'd love to see the guest list the day you tell him you're getting married."

Dale came by, delivered the drinks, and announced he had an emergency in the kitchen, so he left them alone in the corner. "How about you? No wedding plans in your future?"

"This isn't another attempt to ask me about Paula, is it?"

"We're at a party so you have to answer me and not be snarky about it."

She laughed at Sam's finger, which she had pointed in her face. "At the moment I'm a perpetual dater, but it doesn't ever work out."

"Why not?" Sam asked with a smile around her fork.

Her parents were still on the dance floor, and she couldn't remember a time when they acted any differently toward each other. In a time when most marriages and relationships failed, her parents' relationship grew stronger by the day. She never begrudged them their happiness, but it was like they'd sucked up all the luck as far as finding love for themselves and left none for her and Dale. It was a greedy, immature thought, but it did run through her head at times.

"Until I find that, what's the point?" she said, pointing to her parents. "Life with either of them would've driven me crazy by now, but they're each other's perfect match."

"You don't believe there's a perfect match for you somewhere in the world?" Sam asked, her eyes fixed on her plate.

"If there is, they've lost my number, because I haven't come anywhere close to finding them." She scooped up a large cracker full of Dale's shrimp dip and shoved it in her mouth as a way to force herself to stop talking. If she didn't know better, she'd swear Dale had put truth serum in the dip.

The idiotic move to silence herself obviously wasn't lost on Sam because she asked, "Am I making you uncomfortable?"

"You do have a way of making me talk about stuff that normally I wouldn't share with anyone except maybe Dale. But now that you've dragged all my secrets out of me, how about you? What special guy is Ms. Samantha waiting for?"

"I have a list, actually, and until all my demands have been met, I'm not caving on any proposals." Sam's smile was infectious, and its appearance signaled that perhaps Sam was tweaking her a little.

"This ought to be good. Let's hear it."

"I'll give you the first one so as to not bore you," Sam

said, and scooped up another cracker of shrimp dip and handed it to her. "Whoever's interested can't come up to my place for anything until they show up at my window with a mariachi band that can play Billy Joel's 'Just the Way You Are.' That's the first of eighty things on my list."

"Flowers won't cut it, huh?" Chili put her elbows on the table so she could rest her chin on her hands to listen to whatever Sam said. It was fascinating.

"Flowers are a good icebreaker, but the only way to get to the next level is the mariachi band."

She accepted another cracker from Sam and laughed. "So you're telling me you'd have sex with someone who sends you flowers and shows up at your house with a pack of Mexican men in costume? That's kind of kinky."

"Who said anything about sex? I'm talking about a short night consisting of a drink and conversation. Sex comes after the eightieth item."

"Eighty things that build on a mariachi band singing Billy Joel? You must either still be a virgin or have sex every ten years or so. At your age that means there must only be one lucky but broken guy out there with an ice bag on his crotch."

Sam moved on to the fish entree Dale had made and offered Chili a forkful. "You seem awfully interested in my sex life or lack of one, and actually the list came as a result of some bad experiences with some idiots along the way."

"The future Mr. Sam Pellegrin has to pay for the sins of the past, huh? Makes sense, and no matter what, you shouldn't bend on that long-ass list you got going." She decided to reciprocate and scooped up some of Dale's specialty pasta and offered it to Sam. The afternoon was starting to get interesting, but it wouldn't last, since the song had ended and her mom was on her way over.

"Did you see your grandmother's expression?" Joni Alexander asked when she sat down and ate an oyster off Chili's plate. "The last forty years of my life have been worth it just for that."

"Mom, you need to stop hoping Grandma will accept you and get some other goal in this life. And this is Sam Pellegrin, before you start using curse words to describe my grandmother to an invited guest who doesn't know you're joking when you say you hired a killer to take Granny out."

Her mom laughed but didn't appear too upset at having spilled the not-so-hidden family secret. "Nice to meet you, Sam, and thank you for coming."

"Are you having a good time aside from making your nemesis look like she's sucking on a lemon?" Chili asked.

"You and your brother are the best things that God has ever gifted me with, aside from your father, so thank you for all of this. Y'all outdid yourselves this time. It's been a great ride so far, and I'm looking forward to a minimum of another sixty or seventy years, as long as you throw us a good party. Today reminds me of our wedding. It's a shame you and Dale missed that."

Her mom jumped up at hearing her name and excused herself a minute when a new set of guests arrived.

"I take it your dad's mom never took to her."

"I think the fact that I was in a way present at her and dad's wedding had something to do with it, but she's never admitted to it. To this day my mother insists I was the only nine-pound preemie ever born in the state of Louisiana, and my grandmother thinks she did it to trap my father into a life he really didn't want. In Granny's mind my dad was destined for greater things than his career in the oilfield."

"Is that where you get your will to win at all costs?" Sam asked, and Chili wanted to flick the remainder of her plate on Sam's head.

"I've never done anything unethical to win an election. Not that I'm perfect," she said, and moved her chair back a little, "but most of my mistakes have come in my personal life, not in any election."

"I'm sorry, Chili." Sam slid closer, as if to make up for the slight barrier Chili had tried to create. "It wasn't a very good one, but I was joking. My dad has preached to me for a long time to follow your lead when it came to ethics. The profession we're in has very little left, if you ask the average person, but I've admired you and my father for a long time because you've never compromised for the sake of an election outcome."

"I'm sure Huey will take over your education soon enough, and he's the guy who taught me almost everything I know."

"Almost everything?"

"He can't take credit for the question that runs through my head when I first meet with any client." She tried to let the sudden anger go and simply enjoy the party and the fact that Sam was here.

"Not going to share?"

"Before your first solo interview I promise I'll give you a clue." Her mom was looking at them and crooked her finger at her. "Would you excuse me a few minutes?"

"Take your time. I don't want to monopolize your attention."

"You're a lot more pleasant to talk to than my extended family, so don't apologize." Sam laughed, and she almost hated to leave now that they were talking like normal adults who didn't in fact hate each other.

"How does your mom's mother feel about your dad?"

"It took her a few years, but she finally warmed up to him."

"Did she think he wasn't good enough for your mom?" Sam asked, as if wanting to know her whole life story in one afternoon.

"Granny's a devoted Catholic who doesn't like to judge, but in her opinion, good Catholic boys wait, along with the girls they love, until their wedding night. I don't think she's ever forgiven him for making them have to rush a wedding."

"What did she think about Paula?"

"The same thing she thinks about using quantum physics to balance her checkbook."

Sam's eyebrows came together as if she was confused. "Your grandmother uses quantum physics in everyday life?"

"No, and she doesn't know anything about Paula either," she said, and winked before going to see what her mother wanted.

❖

Sam watched Chili walk across the room and noticed how most of the people in her path stopped her, if only to say hello. Her dad had insisted that she attend a few events with him, and when Chili was present, Sam always saw the same thing. Chili seemed to put out some kind of pheromone that made people want to be around her, as if she were some kind of pied piper. Chili's uncanny knack for remembering names also impressed her, especially when it made whoever she was talking to puff up like a peacock on steroids as soon as Chili addressed them.

Her father had told her plenty about Chili, including his warning to stay away from her, but he'd never mentioned how lucky they were Chili was still at the firm. By now Chili should've moved on and used the contacts she had to catapult up to heading the national campaigns that eventually carried you to the promised land—a presidential run. Virgil was, in Sam's opinion, way beneath Chili's talents, but hell if she didn't give him the same attention she had everyone else's campaign they'd ever handled.

"Are you here with Chili?" an attractive older woman asked when she sat down with a glass of champagne.

"Yes, I'm Sam Pellegrin," she said, holding her hand out to the woman.

"Eleanor Alexander, Chili's grandmother," Eleanor said before taking a large sip of her drink. "I'm surprised she brought anyone to this shindig."

"Really, why?" The way Eleanor had said it made her want to side with Chili's mom when it came to this woman. "Chili's a pretty social person, from what I can see."

"As long as our families have had to come together because of the choices my son has made, I've never seen her bring anyone to anything. To see you here is a change that makes me wonder what the future holds."

Sam watched as Chili took her mother's hand and headed out to the dance floor, both with huge smiles. She didn't want to insult Eleanor, but the woman spoke with a distinctive sarcastic edge that was starting to annoy her. In her experience grandparents were loving people who doted and spoiled you rotten. "Mr. Alexander's choices, from what I can see, are better than most. He seems very happy, and he has a beautiful family that loves him. As for Chili, I can't explain why she always attends family functions alone. Maybe she's afraid to subject anyone to her family's views."

"I take it you have no children."

She shook her head at Eleanor's statement.

"I have four sons, and every one of them is divorced but one, so you're right. My son's happy and his family loves him."

"You should tell him that every so often."

Eleanor laughed and took her hand. "For an invited guest you certainly are opinionated. Did Chili paint me as the wicked side of the family who hates her mother?"

"I work with her, and I'm sorry to say, but she never really talks about her family. So my slate is clean as far as any of the Alexanders are concerned. Are you the wicked grandmother who doesn't care for her mother?" she asked with a smile.

"I'm a widow who's happy to see this day."

"What, their wedding anniversary?"

"That too." Eleanor laughed again. "Chili's mother is as passionate a woman as I am, so we'll always be oil and water, but she's given me the greatest gifts any woman could hope for.

Chili and Dale are my only grandchildren, and they're both a lot of fun."

Sam nodded as she placed her other hand over Eleanor's. "Thanks for sharing that with me, but I'm not sure why you did."

"I sat over there and watched you and Chili share a meal, and it made me want to come and introduce myself. Hopefully the next generation will see me as the fun grandmother."

"Did that title go to Chili's other grandmother in this generation?"

"I think we shared that role, but there was too much tension for too many years, and it tainted so many things."

Sam wished her bladder would shrink a few sizes so she could excuse herself and hide in the bathroom, but she wasn't that lucky. Eleanor seemed to want to unburden years of pent-up emotion on someone, and she'd picked that winning lottery number. "Chili's my boss, Mrs. Alexander, and she's a really cool person who I'm sure loves you. Whatever happened, you should put that in the past and enjoy the person she's become." The advice sounded good, and with any luck Eleanor would move on and leave her to watch Chili move around the dance floor.

"I know that, and I apologize for probably sharing more about our history than you wanted to hear, but I wanted to introduce myself and tell you not to be afraid of what's in your heart."

Great. The old lady fancied herself a candidate for an operator's job for the psychic hotline as well with that deep statement. "I'm not sure I know what you're talking about?"

"I see how you look at her, and more importantly how she looks at you. Demand things of my granddaughter, and this will be you a few years down the road," Eleanor said as she waved her hand around the room. "You might think me a meddling old woman, but I want to see Chili this happy one day, and you're a step in that direction."

"I'm not someone she feels that way about, ma'am, but I'm sure one day you'll get your wish."

"That's the fear talking for you, and you've got more spunk than that." Eleanor finished her drink and stood. "I think it's time for you to go cut in." She pointed to Chili and her mother. "It's a party. You're supposed to have fun."

If she'd had more than one glass of wine she could blame the confusing conversation on the alcohol, but she hadn't finished the drink Dale had brought her. Before she could try to start deciphering the uninvited tidbits of information, Chili came back and held her hand out to her.

"Can I have this dance?"

Eleanor flew out of her head as Chili led her around the dance floor, and they stayed there when the music changed to a slower-tempo romantic number. "Thanks for inviting me," she said as she rested her head on Chili's shoulder.

"I'm glad you came," Chili whispered back. "What deep, dark secrets did my grandmother share with you while my mother showed me what a bad dancer I am?"

"If I tell you it won't be a deep, dark secret, but I'll give you a hint. She really does like your mom a little bit, since she's the only daughter-in-law that's lasted."

"You mean she spent time on that and not only how wonderful she thinks I am? My weekly dinners with her have been a waste then."

Sam laughed and slapped Chili's other shoulder. "My God, you're an egomaniac, and she did tell me how wonderful you are. That's why we were arguing when you walked up. I was trying to set her straight on a few things."

"What's the next thing on your list?" Chili said as she pulled back a little so she could see her face.

"The mariachi band wasn't enough to make you think I'm crazy?"

"Of course I think you're crazy, but I'm still curious as to what's the next item."

"A picnic somewhere I would think is romantic." She smiled

up at Chili and thought about shooting the DJ if the song they were dancing to ended anytime soon.

"No hints as to what you think is romantic?"

"If someone is interested enough they'll guess, taking into account how well they know me."

"You should write books on challenge dating," Chili said as she moved them more toward the corner to get out of the crush of the crowd.

"Do you think it would make people want to date more?" she asked as she straightened Chili's collar even though it didn't really need it. "Or would they run away fast?"

"Depends, I guess."

"On?" She asked as the song ended but Chili didn't let her go, and she wanted to cheer when another slow one started.

"If the prize at the end of the list is worth it to undergo the date challenge."

Chili held her closer and waited for this song to end before walking her back to their table. The day had certainly turned out much differently than her usual eating ice cream on her sofa with her cat, and for that she was grateful.

They talked some more after Dale joined them, and Sam stood along with everyone else as the siblings toasted their parents after a few funny stories. This was certainly a different family setting than her usual time with her father, aunt, and both sets of grandparents. Compared to the Alexanders, her family was mild and quiet. Seeing Chili in the middle of all these people made her even more curious about Paula and how Chili had ever spent any time with someone like that. It didn't compute now that she knew that Chili was this loved and actually spent a lot of time with her family.

"Thanks again for inviting me," she said a few hours later as Chili walked her to her car. "I had a great time."

"Thank *you* for agreeing to come with me. I was the envy of all my cousins."

"You owe me a few favors then," she said as she dug her keys out of her purse.

"You can collect whenever you like," Chili said, then fell silent when Sam's phone started ringing.

"Hey, Daddy," Sam said, and reached for Chili's hand when she turned to leave. "Sorry, I'll be a few minutes late, but I'm on my way." She ended the call and tried to decide if now was the time to ask Chili if her father had in fact talked to her about staying away from her.

"Sorry if I've made you late for anything," Chili said, not letting go of Sam's hand.

"My aunt Fern is in town and Dad wanted to take us out to dinner. I actually forgot all about it."

"Get going then before your uncle Tulip decides to show up," Chili said, and laughed.

"Can I ask you something before you go?" Eleanor's warning to not let her fear stand in her way suddenly made sense.

"I met Paula at a campaign early on in my career, and she didn't like to be ignored. After coming on to me with the subtlety of a Mack truck, I gave in, and after that idiotic move, the real Paula emerged." Chili stared at what Sam guessed was her shoes and appeared so uncomfortable Sam almost stopped her from finishing. "When I broke it off to save myself from any more of her insanity, she made a scene in the middle of our candidate's headquarters. It didn't leave anyone there with any doubt to what kind of relationship we'd had and what she thought of me in every sense, both in and out of bed."

"Why tell me after all this time? And for the record, that wasn't what I intended to ask you."

"You really wanted to know, and I didn't tell you before because Paula's at the top of my list of embarrassments. If we're going to work together I didn't see the wisdom in denying you the answer to any question you ask. Keeping it from you might give you the impression I don't trust you." Chili finally glanced up at her and shrugged. "But having said that unnecessarily, what's your question?"

"Did my father talk to you about me? I mean about something other than work?"

"If I answer that truthfully, it'll make me sound like a twelve-year-old who's whining, and if I don't answer, we're back in that no-trust territory. So how about you cut me some slack on this one?"

"I don't want to know so I can go back and yell at him, but you really put some distance between us the last couple of weeks, and I didn't want you to think I had something to do with it if he did." She stepped closer to Chili and took her hands. "I worked so hard to graduate early so I could work with you. I have from the time my father hired you, and I don't want his misconceptions about you to cloud whatever relationship we're going to have."

"I apologize for that, so don't blame Huey. Sometimes I'm not sure how to handle situations so I back off until something comes to me."

"Was the situation this time me?"

"Sort of, but how about we start over in the morning and we'll see where that gets us?"

"I can accept that," she said, and squeezed Chili's hands. "Can I ask you one more thing and have you not think I'm totally crazy?"

"I might have to go home and lie down afterward, but go ahead."

"Whatever we start over tomorrow, can we keep it to ourselves and leave Huey out of it?"

"We'll see," Chili said, and let her go to open her door. "Now get going so you don't keep Aunt Petunia waiting."

"It's Aunt Fern."

"Then I might start calling you Petunia since you're not a boring green plant. Have fun and thanks for the afternoon. Drive safe."

CHAPTER NINE

As they continued their work on the Emery campaign, Sam noticed that while everyone had specific tasks to do, ever since their unplanned date, she worked with Chili every day overseeing the whole process. For once she was glad she'd kept quiet when Chili had asked what she'd learned at Tulane to get her degree. From Virgil's wardrobe change to his improved message, she realized Chili was a better teacher than any class she'd sat in.

It was like Virgil was a puzzle that Chili had torn to pieces and put back together in a way that made for a more appealing picture, though she hadn't really changed any of the original parts. The first debate between the candidates from all accounts had gone to Virgil, and he'd cut his opponent's lead to less than two points in the polls.

The only drawback to their new and better work relationship was that after the day of her parents' anniversary party, Chili hadn't brought up anything else remotely personal. If she hadn't been there, Sam would've thought she'd conjured the whole thing up, and she wanted to see that side of Chili again.

"What do we have on tap for tomorrow?" Sam asked as they sat in Chili's office at eleven o'clock at night. The muted lighting made it possible to see the ships passing by on the river, but Chili was more involved in the political blogs she loved to visit than in her or the pretty view. Despite all the effort they'd put into Virgil, he was small potatoes in the realm of what they did, but the big campaigns were close and it was time to start putting out bait.

She was sure at least one major campaign was theirs since Chili spent a minimum of a couple of hours on the phone with Rooster every day. The prostitution scandal was mentioned once a week in the news, and that was building up Rooster's chances as a good alternative, so Chili had her and the rest of the team construct Rooster's message that had been distributed to all the media. It wasn't a stretch to paint him as a solid real difference that'd bring honor and dignity back to the office Fudge had smeared with smut and mud, as one older gentleman she'd talked to had told her.

"The chamber invited Virgil to come back for a question-and-answer session for their monthly lunch tomorrow. Then there's a town-hall meeting tomorrow at the Assembly Center."

"The chamber again? That must mean we're moving even higher in the polls. They don't invite if they smell a losing campaign."

Chili clicked off local politics and opened some national pages. "Virgil's come a long way, and unless he's got some deep, dark secret I don't know about, he should be able to squeak this one out."

"The only secret we have to worry about is anyone finding out about his mother's penchant for rhinestone-studded clothing. Thankfully she was as open to a makeover as her son was when we met him," Sam said, remembering the expression on Virgil's mother's face when she came out of the dressing room in what she'd called the drabbest suit in the world.

"I'm sure her Election Night outfit will be memorable. She's got to be in withdrawal by now."

"Are you going to kick me upstairs for the next round of campaigns?"

Apparently not hearing the question, Chili leaned forward,

completely engrossed in what she was reading. After her talk with her father about what wouldn't make her happy, Sam got up every morning and gave herself a pep talk before going in to work. Chili hadn't really opened up to her any more, but she did seem relaxed around her, which made Sam crave more.

Chili was over-the-top professional, and she also took the time to compliment Sam on something daily that didn't really have a lot to do with work. When Chili did, it was the only time in their workday that Sam indulged in noticing things about Chili that would kill her father if he could read her mind.

"Think you've earned that spot already, have you? Are you secretly sitting for your portrait in the lobby?"

Chili's usually short hair had gotten shaggy and was curling toward her ears, and Sam had the urge to run her fingers through it and comb it back. Unlike Paula, though, whose presence Chili could usually sense when she was within a mile of her, she hadn't gotten any kind of over-the-top rise out of Chili aside from the day she got thrown out of her car.

"I would've thought you'd had enough of me." Sitting in one of the comfortable chairs in Chili's office she kicked off her pumps and put her feet up.

"Of course no…" Chili's voice died away slowly before she finished the word as she stared at Sam's feet. The red toenail polish was the only thing Sam could think that might make the blank look appear on Chili's face. Intriguing response, she thought.

"You do want to get rid of me then?" she asked as she put both feet on the ground. Perhaps Chili was paying more attention to her than she thought.

"Of course not—that's what I meant." Chili was talking, but her eyes never left Sam's feet.

Slowly Sam slipped her shoes back on and almost laughed at the frown that turned just the corners of Chili's lips downward. "It's getting late, boss. Are you ready to head home?"

"I just have a few more things left, but if you want I could skip them and we could grab a drink or something."

It was like someone had fired a starter pistol and Chili had suddenly come to life in a way Sam wanted, but rushing now would only give Chili the wrong idea. Not that she was taking anything her father had said into consideration, but more what Maria had told her. If she wanted more, it'd not only have to be different from what Chili was used to, but she'd have to work to whip up Chili's need for more. She didn't intend to be another notch in Chili's bedpost.

"Not tonight, but thanks for asking." She stood and bent to pick up her purse. No, if she wanted to get Chili's attention, she was going to have to use more than just toenail polish.

"Wait up and I'll walk you to your car. It's pretty late."

"Anything special you want me to do tomorrow?" she asked as Chili locked the door.

"Beth's taking care of the media spots that center around coastal issues for the coming week, and I've got everyone else on the mail-outs Virgil wants. They're not the most effective, but they don't hurt. That frees us up to have lunch with the chamber tomorrow, unless you've got other plans."

"Sounds good to me. Who in their right mind would pass up an intimate lunch for six hundred people?"

"Not any woman in her right mind," Chili said, and smiled.

Sam was starting to get addicted to that open, relaxed expression on Chili. When Chili smiled or laughed, her attractiveness doubled. "Do you need me to save you from Paula tomorrow?"

"She's going with Candy to the Junior League's luncheon that's at the same time, to answer questions about Virgil's views about women. After Paula met Candy, she must have slipped a drug into her drink to make her consider the friendship they share." The weather had changed from the warm morning to temperatures in the forties after a driving rain.

The wind coming off the river was starting to make Sam shiver, so as much as she didn't want to, she needed to send Chili on her way. "Stay warm and I'll see you tomorrow."

Chili was staring at her as if she was trying to read between the lines of what she was saying. Anyone Chili had showed interest in was probably naked in the back of her car by now, but that was never going to happen with her, even with the mariachi band and a thousand picnics. "You sure you don't have time for a drink?"

"It's late, and I can use all the beauty sleep I can get."

"Opinions might vary on that. Any more beautiful and you might get to be too distracting," Chili said as she opened her door and waved her into the car. "See you tomorrow."

"Uh-huh," she said, and closed her door before she compromised anything because of hormones. "I actually have a little sympathy for Paula now that I have time to think about it," she said as she drove out of the lot. All she had to worry about now was where Chili was headed since she didn't seem ready to go home.

"Take a wrong turn on the yellow brick road home, and I'm hitting you with my car," she said into her rearview mirror when Chili turned to head downtown.

❖

"Can I have your autograph?" Chili asked when Sophie Grossman opened her hotel room door.

"How in the hell did you get up here?" Sophie said as she opened her arms to Chili. "I stayed at the Piquant because of their great security."

"I scaled up the side of the building and smashed through the window because I had a burning desire to see you. Want to head downstairs to the bar before the tabloids start spreading false rumors about you if they see you with a devastatingly good-looking woman in your room?" Chili kissed Sophie's cheek and stepped back into the hallway.

"You sure you're not too tired?" Sophie grabbed a small purse and took her arm as they walked to the elevator. "And I'm not going anywhere with you if you don't tell me something about Samantha Pellegrin."

"How do you know anything about Sam? Never mind. I don't want to know if you're still talking to my mother." She waved to the waiter when they got to the bar, and the guy showed them to a table in the crowded room full of people listening to the live music.

"Your mother loves her already, and she only talked to her for a nanosecond. And before you start yelling, all your dear mother wants is for you to be happy." Sophie laughed when she pouted. "Stop channeling a three-year-old and listen to me. Don't act like you don't care about the future when it comes to anything but politics. When you're old and sick, Rooster and his wife aren't going to give a crap about you." Sophie grabbed her chin and made her look her in the eye. "I'm being serious. You're going to throw away every chance at what you need in your life unless someone threatens you."

"Are you here to threaten me constantly or for a visit?"

"I'm here for a story, actually, since one of your senators can't get a pretty girl to talk to him unless he's got a twenty between his teeth. The network wants me to do a story starting with what the average Joe who voted for him thinks all the way up to the hallowed halls of the United States Senate." Sophie held her glass up in a toast. "Since you're representing Rooster, I'm guessing you're not going to be too upset about that. Do you want any part of what I report?"

"You know how much I love being in front of the camera, and for something like this it does make my job easier, but if I participate it makes me look like a spoiled child trying to get her way no matter the cost. I'll help you with anything behind the scenes, but it's best if whatever you find isn't tainted by his opponent's campaign people in the next election."

Sophie poked her in the shoulder and laughed. "I expected you to say that, but I had to ask, so now we've got nothing to talk about except your girlfriend."

"Let's not start planning my wedding yet, and I'm not giving you any information on Sam that you'll use later in collaboration with my mother." She paid the bill and wanted to go home. The long day had picked that moment to kick her in the ass. "You set for tomorrow?"

"Are you?" Sophie finished her drink and stood up. "I have a source that tells me the randy senator is going to make an appearance at the chamber luncheon tomorrow. It's his way of trying to rebuild his credibility as well as testing the waters of how easily he blushes now that his little secret is out."

"If that's true, Virgil's going to get lost in the shuffle." She kissed Sophie's cheek and glanced at her watch. It was late, but she had no choice but to go back to the office and make some calls. "Can you make it upstairs okay?"

"I'll say yes if you tell me what's going through that brain of yours."

"Don't jinx me, sweet pea, but if I can work a little magic tonight it'll make your story more interesting tomorrow." The drive back was quick since the Mardi Gras parade scheduled for that night had ended and taken the crowds with it.

"Do you care who wins the state senatorial race in special election at the end of this month?" she asked when Rooster answered his cell.

"Is this some new service you're offering on nights you can't sleep? It's after midnight, Chili, in case you've lost track of the time."

"Trust me, I'd rather be in bed counting votes, but it's important."

"As long as whoever it is won't be as big a scumbag as the

guy who just went to jail, I really don't have any problem with the outcome."

She picked up the campaign pin Virgil's mother had made her as a joke and smiled. It had rhinestones around Virgil's picture. Its twin was the one little bit of bling Virgil's mother wore on the campaign trail every day. "How would you like to come to New Orleans tomorrow to endorse Virgil?"

"I'd want to do this why? Aside from you asking me, that is?" Rooster asked.

She explained her reasoning as she searched through the phone book for mariachi bands. When she didn't find a section in the yellow pages, she tried Google. "Will I see you tomorrow?"

"You want to write up my endorsement statement, or do you want me to do it?"

"I'll email you as soon as I finish it." She wrote down the phone number she found at the second link she'd clicked on.

"Anything else I can do for you now that I'm wide awake?"

"If you had to plan a romantic picnic where would you go?"

"Virgil asked for that too?" Rooster asked, and laughed. "If he needs to know that, tell him I'm not endorsing him."

"Call it research on my part."

"I'd tell you, but since I don't know what the girl's definition of romance is, you need to do what you do best and figure it out." She wrote Rooster's brief comments and reread them before sending them on. "Did you hear me?"

"What do you think I do best?" she asked to humor him.

"Homework. It's the secret to your success and the reason old farts like me chase you around until you say yes to representing us."

"Go back to sleep, old fart. I need you to be sharp and charming tomorrow." She hung up and made a few more calls as she continued her Internet searches. When she turned the lights off for the second time, she'd done all she could for Virgil, but she had more than that on her mind. She stared at the building and wondered what it would be like not to come here every day.

"If I show up at Samantha's window with a band to get into Huey's little girl's apartment, he's going to blackball me so fast I'll be lucky if my shadow will keep up to make it out the door with me."

❖

"Did you decide on anything?" Rooster asked as they stood outside the New Orleans Convention Center's largest ballroom waiting to get into their monthly luncheon. With Senator Billy Fudge's announcement that he'd be there, the number of people attending had doubled so there'd been a change in venue, but that only worked in Virgil's and Rooster's favor.

"Decide on what?" she asked as she scanned the crowd in front and back of them looking for Sam. It wasn't like her to be late, and they'd left the office at the same time.

"Picnic locations," Carla said, as she hung on to Rooster's arm and smiled. Despite their age differences and her inexperience when it came to campaigning, Carla had the smile and manners down pat. She was going to be a major asset to them when they finally began in earnest. "Who's the lucky lady?"

Chili saw Sam heading toward them with Sophie and her crew following closely behind, Maria and another crew not that far up in the procession line. "I'll tell you later, and if either of you brings this up in front of anyone, I don't care who, I quit. Make that I quit right after I punch you in the nose."

"No need for any more hints," Carla said, making Rooster give her a confused look, so she whispered in his ear.

"I see a shotgun in your future," Rooster said in a gleeful singsong voice.

"Shut up," she said as she waved to Sam and shook her head

at both Sophie and Maria. "Keep walking, you two. We don't have any comments."

"I haven't asked you or Rooster anything," Maria said as Sophie kept walking after smiling at her. "Makes me think you're hiding something."

"Hiding something?" Chili laughed. "You've seen the guest list for today, haven't you? If we're hiding something we're pure amateurs in comparison."

"Can I quote you?"

"Sure, and the next time I have something going on I'll call that girl from channel four. She likes me more than you do."

"I bet," Sam said, so Chili stopped teasing Maria. "Daddy called and said he was inside already and had purchased a couple of tables, so we don't have to worry about finding a place to sit."

"Why not sit with him and Virgil, along with whoever else he invited, and I'll take Rooster, Carla, and the rest of the staff to the other table," Chili said to Sam quietly as the line moved up.

"Why?" Sam pointed to a large palm near the glass front of the building. "Will you guys hold our place?" Sam asked Carla and Rooster.

"We'd be happy to, and we'll check you in on the chance you're longer than you think," Carla said.

"We'll be right back." Chili followed Sam, with Carla and Rooster laughing behind her. "What's wrong?" she asked Sam as they stood under the plant, which in no way was hiding them from the onlooking crowd. "You okay?"

"Why don't you want to sit with me?" Sam's expression was so sad Chili would've thought she was asking why she'd given her puppy away to bad people.

"I believe you said something about keeping Huey out of the loop when it came to anything regarding us starting over. Why make him worry if we don't have to?"

"That's all?" Sam pulled on the button of Chili's jacket as well as stared at it.

"Sure. Why, what did you think?" She fought the urge to touch Sam's face.

"Nothing." In Chili's opinion Sam tried her best to smile as she finally lifted her head.

"You don't sound too convincing."

"I thought turning you down last night might've made you change your mind."

Chili gave in to the craving to feel Sam's skin under her fingers but decided on moderation by tapping the end of her nose. "I told you I'm a little slow, but I remember the rules."

"Rules," Sam said, her smile more relaxed and genuine. "You need the parameters of rules to be nice to someone?"

"I was talking about that list of yours. I jumped the gun last night, so don't worry that we're headed in the wrong direction."

"Does that mean we're headed in a dating direction then?" Sam asked, but didn't appear upset about the possibility.

"I'm not sure that's what you want, but I should've known better before just asking you out for a drink. If you're not interested, I'll keep you company until Mr. Right comes along to sweep you off your feet," she said, giving Sam an out.

"I'm not saying that's not what I want."

"Sam…Chili," Huey said, loud enough from where Carla and Rooster were standing to interrupt them. "Is there a problem?" he asked as he joined them.

"Sam was giving me an update on something I asked her to do and didn't want to be overheard with all this press around. Is something going on inside?" Chili asked, ready to walk away.

"No." Huey glanced between them as if not knowing what to say next. "It just looks bad that you're over here ignoring our clients."

"We're done," she said, and laughed at the absurdity of the situation. Her curiosity about Sam was taking her back to her high-school days when she had to skulk around to spend time with her girlfriend. Back then it was the same issue of unaccepting parents. She hadn't cared for it then, and it was starting to get to her now. "Was there anything else, Sam?"

"There's a little more, but it can wait until we get back to the office. Come on, Daddy. Let's make sure our clients find their seats without getting lost or developing a personality disorder from our rudeness." Sam grabbed Huey's bicep and dragged him away as she glanced back at Chili.

"I'm not telling you your business, Chili, but be careful how you go about this. There's nothing worse in this world than an overprotective angry daddy," Rooster said as Carla lifted their joined hands and kissed his knuckles.

"He should know. The first time I brought him home to meet mine, it made me glad he's still so spry," Carla said, and laughed as Rooster joined in. "But he's right. Don't do this unless you're serious about where you're going. Considering who it is, don't try for the Sunday drive only to forget how to drive the next day. Understand?"

"For once I'm not sure what I'm doing, so thanks for the advice."

"That's actually a step in the right direction when it comes to you. From what I've seen since we've met, you usually drive at warp speed, and your brakes come on just as fast," Carla said as they finally reached the sign-in desk.

"Enough of the driving analogies. Let's get in there."

Once everyone sat down, Chili almost choked on her iced tea when Billy Fudge walked to the microphone and asked everyone to lower their head in prayer. Granted, the Lord was the definition of forgiveness, but the general public took a few months to forget, much less forgive when you were spending their tax dollars on hookers. The first heckler who screamed, "Are you kidding me" was sitting somewhere in the middle of the large, cavernous room, and it prompted the others who were just as disgusted to yell out their frustration.

"Please, everyone, I'm trying to bless our meal," Billy said, and Chili couldn't help but laugh when a shower of salad that was already on the table fell on Fudge as he called for calm. In all her years of attending events like this, it was the first time she'd ever been witness to a one-sided food fight.

All hell broke loose after that, and the bread and dessert followed until the state police present had to escort the senator out. Sophie and her crew, as well as Maria and hers, were in great position to film him covering his head to keep from getting hit with anything else as he ran for the exit. His suit and his head were dripping with a mixture of chocolate cake, butter, and the hot bacon dressing the spinach salad was drenched in.

The president and executive director of the chamber were at the podium waving their hands for quiet and decorum. "What in the hell was that?" Rooster said as he wiped tears of laughter from his eyes.

"A warning to you to not hire any prostitutes when you get elected. I'll be right back, so don't do anything to turn the mob against you." The staff was busy resetting the room, so Chili took the opportunity to step back outside but stopped to talk to Sophie when Sophie called her name. "I'm sure you got all you needed to make the story all you want it to be, so I've got nothing to add."

"You don't need to comment. I just wanted you to stop," Sophie said as she glanced over Chili's shoulder at something. "I'm going to have to skip dinner tonight so try to find something else to occupy yourself with. Maybe later on this week we can reschedule, but my sweetie's coming in tonight to set up a series on Fudge. It'll consist of a few segments with the slant on what's wrong with American politics, with him as the poster boy."

"Since you were looking forward to good seafood, go ahead and use our reservations at GW Fins tonight. It's a good place to romance someone, so good luck." She kept walking and glanced back before stepping into the lobby. From Sam's expression, Huey had taken the opportunity to tell her exactly what kind of relationship she and Sophie had shared. "Sure he did, since it'll be one more thing that'll make this harder than it has to be," she murmured to herself.

❖

"God, I'm an idiot," Sam said loudly in the comfort of her car. Her father had almost gleefully told her about the hot times Chili had shared with Sophie Grossman and that it had ended only because of Sophie's promotion. From the way the news slut was eyeing Chili, she had more than an interview in mind, and Chili had stood there like a horn dog nodding like she couldn't wait.

Sam arrived at her town house in uptown area and hit the steering wheel with her fist after she turned the ignition off. Chili hadn't come back to the office after the luncheon; Sam had waited until after three, then finally given up and gone home. "What the hell was I thinking?" she asked herself. "Being in any kind of relationship with her isn't like waiting for the other shoe to drop on a constant basis. It's like being clubbed half to death with the shoe every day."

The man tapping on her window scared her enough to scream. "Are you Samantha Pellegrin?" he asked, holding a large bouquet in the crook of his other arm.

"Yes," she said, not lowering her window or opening her door. He appeared harmless enough, but she didn't want to be the first gullible person to be mugged by a guy pretending to deliver flowers. It was way before Lent, but she was giving up gullibility this year instead of chocolate, like her grandmother always hinted at.

He held up the card that came with the flowers and pointed out his delivery truck as if to convince her he wasn't there to rob her blind. "If you lower your window a little I'll give you this." He tapped the note on the window this time.

She did and reached for the card that had her name written outside in handwriting she recognized. It was surprising how fast she could lose her anger.

> *You probably missed it on the national news, but Sophie Grossman is engaged to one of her producers and is blissfully happy. Granted, we were close at one time, but I'm happy for her and wish her the best. These flowers, though, are not to announce Sophie's good fortune, but just a way to let you know I was thinking about you. If that freaks you out a little, then I'll send flowers to everyone else in the office to express what a good job I think you're all doing and you simply got yours first.*
> *Chili*

She grabbed a bill from her wallet before opening the door and apologized for keeping the guy waiting. "How many are in that?" she asked, pointing to the arrangement as he followed her upstairs after insisting she keep her money and carrying them for her. Chili had sent the flowers and had given him a healthy tip, he'd told her.

"Three dozen pink roses," he said, and stood outside her door until she invited him in and patted the spot where he could put them down. "Can I ask a question? You don't have to answer if you don't want to."

"Sure," she said, wondering where this was going.

"Are you in any way related to Chili?" The guy put the arrangement down and made sure every flower was perfect. It was a humorous sight since he resembled a grizzly bear.

"No. Why do you ask?"

"In all the time she's done business with us, she's only ordered these, albeit in smaller numbers, for three other women."

She snorted and stared at the guy, wondering if he had some

kind of grudge against Chili. "Aren't you messing up her game by sharing that with me? If she's been a longtime customer that's kind of rude, even if I appreciate the heads-up."

"I doubt she wants to date her two grandmothers and her mother, ma'am. That's why I asked. You're the first person I've ever delivered to that's not related to her."

"Good to know, and thanks for carrying that up for me."

As soon as she'd locked the door behind the guy, she kicked her shoes off and stretched her toes. When she removed her hose, she made sure her toes were still as perfect as when she'd left the pedicurist that morning and wondered if the new color would be as interesting to Chili as the other one was. It was still in the red family, but she'd gone a little darker this time.

"Thank you for the lovely surprise today," she said after Chili's message had played. "Totally unnecessary, but they're beautiful."

She was disappointed Chili hadn't picked up, but after what had happened at lunch she was probably stuck in meetings with both Virgil and Rooster. From the crowd's reaction when Rooster stood up to deliver his endorsement of Virgil, the business people of New Orleans were ready for change when it came to their senator. That was great for Rooster, but Chili had left without saying good-bye, so that wasn't so great for her. But Chili had sent flowers, which had to mean something. "Maybe Sophie wasn't available so she's hedging her bets."

The phone in her hand rang, startling her so much that she dropped it. She took a deep breath before answering, thinking it was Chili returning her call. "Did you get home without food on your clothing?" Maria asked.

"Did you?"

"I'm sending Fudge my dry-cleaning bill for the sprinkling of salad dressing all over my suit. It was worth it, though, to see that pompous ass covered in such a public display of disapproval." Maria laughed, but Sam still heard people in the background.

"Chili should be thrilled with Sophie's plan to expose Billy for the jerk he is with a series of stories about what happened. She asked me to help out and said she'd include me in the national coverage."

"That's great, I'm happy for you. Did you know they were a couple?"

"If you're talking about Chili and Sophie, yes, but that's been a while ago, and it ended with them remaining friends."

"That's not what my father told me." She was whining but didn't mind showing off her insecurities to Maria.

"Remember, Huey's also the man who planted a big red flag in the center of Chili's forehead as a warning to stay away from her, which in this day and age is kind of feudal-lord thinking. If you want the real scoop on Chili History 101 you can ask me. I don't have any vested interest here other than seeing my pal happy." Maria went on to tell her what had happened, which meant Sophie had stopped Chili earlier just to screw with her. Chili's expression when she'd turned around and looked at Sam was a sure bet Chili knew she'd fallen for Sophie's mind games. It showed a total lack of trust on her part when it came to Chili, and Chili hadn't really done anything to deserve that.

"Guess what I got today?" She ran her finger tip over one of the blossoms and wondered if Chili was sorry she'd sent them.

"A case of rotten fish. From the funk you sound like you're in, that's my best guess."

"Chili sent me flowers."

"Really," Maria said, and paused. "How many and what color?"

"Three dozen pink roses. Why, is there some hidden message I should know about?" She walked to her bedroom and started undressing.

"It screams 'I'm interested,' from what I can tell, so you're in a good position if you really do like her. That part hasn't changed, has it?"

"No, but I keep remembering what you said about her leaving if it doesn't work out."

"Don't blame not wanting to try on me, Sam." Maria moved to somewhere quieter. "Why not try, and if it doesn't work out promise to have sex with her every so often if she agrees to still work for you. That should be benefit enough to stay."

"You're disgusting," she said, but still laughed as something hit her bedroom window. She ignored it, thinking it was a falling acorn from the tree outside that had gotten caught in the wind.

"It's better than giving her a raise, and it'll relax both of you, so what's disgusting about that?"

Something else hit the window so she went to investigate. "Oh my God," she said slowly.

"What?" Maria asked with alarm.

"I'll have to call you back." She hung up even though Maria was yelling at her not to. "I'm not in mortal danger," she said when Maria called back, "but I really do need to go."

"Hot date?" Maria said, and laughed.

"Not yet, but I'm hoping."

CHAPTER TEN

"Y ou're sure, right?"

"Sí, señora. We practiced since last night so we'll do our best."

Chili tried to ignore the slowing cars and pedestrians who'd stopped when they saw the ten-piece mariachi band she'd found to kick-start her social life. It only took a few more hundred-dollar bills to get their boss to take her seriously and learn a Billy Joel song overnight. When she finally wrote her memoirs, this was certainly getting its own chapter.

"She's still up there, right?" she asked the flower-delivery guy.

"I stayed like you asked, and she hasn't come down since I took the flowers up. If she's trying to avoid you I can't vouch that she didn't run out the back door when I wasn't looking."

"All right, smart-ass," she said as she scoured the ground for small pebbles.

"Here, since I'm guessing you're looking for rocks that are outside your head," the guy said with a smile, and dropped a handful of acorns in her palm. "You need to move farther north if you want to recreate one of those movie scenes. Also start praying she's not filling up some big pot of water to drench you with. If those guys get those pretty outfits wet they're going to beat the crap out of you."

"I'm so glad I invited you along for the moral support." She took a deep breath and started tossing the acorns toward the window the guy had pointed out was Sam's. No way could she break the pane with an acorn so she put some heat into her swing. It took only two for the blinds to part a little, but Sam didn't open the window. "You're sure she was alone?" If she looked out her window and saw this spectacle there'd have been more action than Sam had showed so far, unless Sam had company.

"Yep, and she loved the flowers. I'm taking off so I don't make you nervous. My job here is done."

When the blinds went up a few minutes later and Sam opened the window, Chili saw she was wearing a robe. She'd probably been undressed or in her pajamas. That was a relief. "You guys ready?"

The guitarists went first and were soon joined by the trumpet players, and she was surprised to recognize the melody with a distinctive Spanish flair. But the guy in charge didn't know the words, so she took a deep breath and started singing. It was definitely not one of her talents, but Sam wanted the whole package and that's what she was getting, bad vocals and all.

She got through to the end, having memorized the words, and Sam clapped as she bowed. "I suppose you'll want to come up now," Sam said as the band started another song a little quieter than the first. There was a crowd around Chili now, their gazes going from her to Sam as if they were at a tennis match where one of the players was on the second floor. Having so many witnesses would add new meaning to the humiliation of being shot down.

"Maybe later," she said, and a murmur went through the crowd there for that night's parade. "I want you to come down if you're free."

"What do you have in mind?"

"I want to get through the first few things on the list so I can find out what the next couple are."

Sam lost her smile and narrowed her eyes at her. "If you're

checking things off as fast as you can because you think there's some big prize in it for you, pack it up, and thanks for the serenade."

A few women in the audience clapped at Sam's indignation, and the men let out an amused "ooh."

"Do you realize how many mariachi bands in New Orleans know anything by Billy Joel?" she asked, already aggravated. She'd never met a woman who lit the fuse of her temper as fast as Sam did, which made her question her sanity on an hourly basis after hearing about this ridiculous agenda to get a date. "The fact it's the first thing on your list makes me think you know it's none, which saves you from having to commit to any invitations."

"Touchy," a woman close to her said, and Chili took a breath to relax.

"I'm not rushing, and I'm sorry for being rude. Why not come down before you judge my motives?"

Sam stared at her for a few minutes, as if trying to decide if she was going to give in to her invitation. "I have to get dressed, so you want to come up and wait?"

"No, take your time. I'll accept suggestions from the mob while you get ready."

"Just don't take anyone up on any other invitations before I'm dressed." Sam's smile was back, as was her sense of humor. "What should I wear?"

Chili resisted the urge to say earrings and a smile, and from Sam's expression, she could tell Sam could almost read her thoughts. "Surprise me."

❖

Chili opened the car door for Sam after she'd followed her advice about taking her time. Over thirty minutes had passed since Sam had disappeared from the window, and Chili had gotten some ribbing about it from the people there to stake out their parade spot. They'd all clapped when Sam finally made it downstairs dressed in jeans and a sweater, like she was.

"No hints?" Sam asked when she got in and started the car.

"One of the reasons that made me decide on my career path was my love of Louisiana history," she said as she decided not to take St. Charles Avenue, choosing instead a route that would take them through the narrow side streets. "Some of our past is good, some bad, but you have to admit that all of it's interesting."

"If that's your hint, you suck at giving them."

"I'm not completely sure yet, but I think we have a lot in common, which means you might have a love of history as well." She ignored Sam's attempt at humor. "If that's true, it skews your idea of romance, so I started with what I would think was romantic and tweaked it a little."

"If we're picnicking in a lecture hall at Tulane while someone talks about Louisiana history, you're way off." Sam laughed to take the sting out of her words. "No matter what, I'm going to love it since you've gone to all this trouble."

"If you were kidding about the band, now wouldn't be a good time to tell me," Chili said, and turned onto the street that paralleled the port of New Orleans.

"Since you're not good with hints, why don't you tell me why you decided to do this?" Sam turned in the seat so she was facing her, as if to study her reaction when she spoke. So far in all the time they'd spent together Chili got the impression that Sam was sort of a human lie detector. "You haven't admitted it, and Daddy hasn't admitted it, but I'm positive he talked about me to you without my consent. Considering how old I am, I'm sure you can imagine how embarrassing that is, so I hope you don't hold it against me."

"We've known each other awhile now, Sam, and I've watched you from the time you were in high school."

Sam placed her hand on Chili's bicep. "When you put it like that, it makes you sound like some cradle robber. You're really not that much older than me, so please don't tell me this is leading to a more sisterly relationship."

"What I was going to say," she said as she reached for Sam's hand and held it, "is I've never been bored with you. Even when you were that eager high-schooler, you set yourself apart."

"How so?" Sam asked as they stopped at the guard shacks in front of one of the shipping companies.

"I like hearing what's on your mind, and like I said, you don't bore me. My mom always said when she met my dad, it didn't take long for her to wonder what came next. The answer she was looking for was more than what a lot of her friends wanted, like the big wedding and family." She drove forward when the guy waved her through, glad to be able to give Sam her undivided attention when she found a parking spot. "Her explanation is why I've never been really good at relationships."

"*Your* explanation is sorely lacking," Sam said as she pulled on her fingers. "You can tell me anything, Chili. I promise I'll listen."

"My mom has always been a little different than most people, and she views life as not so much a journey but a gift of time. Sort of like if at birth God gifted you with two large containers side by side, and one was filled with perfect colorless stones while the other was empty. Every day that passed, though, time took one stone from the full container and placed it in the empty one. Once that day was used up and placed in the other container, it took on a color. For the not-so-good days, the stones turned gray and dull, but the good days were full of vibrant hues. At the end of her days, when the scales of the containers tip in the other direction and the full one becomes empty, she wants the other container to reflect what she hopes to be a rainbow."

"What a beautiful thought," Sam said.

"To get that variation would be impossible without my father in her life, so she told me to hold out until I find the person who'd fill my life with the color of joy." She shrugged, trying to disguise the discomfort of showing Sam too much of herself. "From our first meeting, I've always wondered what was next for you, and now I'd like to see how I fit into that."

"And my father?"

"I have to balance what I want with what Huey wants, and accept what can happen if I pick wrong."

"What tipped the scales for you?"

She gazed at Sam and admitted, if only to herself, how lucky she or anyone else would be to have this young woman to share a life with. Sam was much more than her beauty, but that part was hard to ignore. Her blond hair streaked with lighter highlights that were painted by the sun, blue eyes, and distinctive features turned heads everywhere. But Chili had had plenty of beautiful women. Sam's heart and intellect made her the complete package.

"You did, Sam," she said as she opened the door and moved to open Sam's before she retrieved a basket, which Dale had put together, from the trunk. "I love my job, but that's all Huey can really take away from me. Unless you agree with him, and want me just as a friend, I want to wonder what comes next."

"A picnic in the least romantic spot in the city," Sam said, and laughed before putting her arm around Chili's waist. "But as long as you don't run off, I'm looking forward to it."

"Have a little faith, Ms. Pellegrin."

The tugboat her friend said would be there was moored with the engines running. Chili had taken this trip numerous times when she needed to clear her head and the boat was making a run. The tug could be operated from the main wheel room or the high flybridge built to have a good line of sight over the barges and loads they hauled, but it also gave a great view over the levees on both sides of the river.

"Are you up for a climb?" Chili asked as one of the crewmen took the basket from her. Sam took her hand without hesitating as they made their way up to the roof of the flybridge. The railing facing forward had been removed, giving them a clear view of the water, and cushions had been set up against the back and deck so they could sit comfortably as they started their cruise north. There was still enough daylight to enjoy some of the grand homes and plantations they'd pass as they made their way to Baton Rouge and back.

"This is incredible," Sam said for what seemed like the hundredth time as she sat close to her and accepted a refill of wine. They were passing a section lined with the ancient oaks that had witnessed the good and bad that had happened along these banks.

The sun had set, so Chili had taken the fleece blanket she'd brought and draped it over both of them after clearing their dinner off to the side. For the first time in her life she was actually courting someone, and it made her laugh when she thought of her mother and what she'd say about this if she decided to share what she'd planned for Sam.

"Thank you for this, Chili," Sam said as she moved closer so they were pressed against each other. "You certainly win when it comes to creativity. This is the most memorable date I've ever been on."

Chili smiled and buried all her lascivious thoughts for the moment. With anyone else, this was where she'd seal the deal, but that's where this would end. If that happened without her trying her best, she instinctively knew she'd experience true regret for the first time in her life and it would last for rest of her life. No, this would be a slow process that involved not only imagination, but a string of cold, lonely showers.

"What are you thinking so hard about?" Sam asked as she slid her hand down her arm until they were holding hands. "You don't turn into a rat at midnight, do you?"

"I hope not, since I don't think pumpkins float well." She

let Sam's hand go so she could put her arm around her. "And I'm thinking about what a great time I'm having."

"You're not scared yet?" Sam squeezed her fingers as she asked, and Chili took it as telegraphing her fear.

"Yes," she said as she encouraged Sam closer. The wind was starting to pick up and the temperature was dropping as they came about and headed back. The return trip wouldn't be as scenic, but with the current, it'd also take half the time, which meant not that much small talk. "I'm actually kind of terrified, if you want the whole truth."

"Can I admit something to you and not have you think I'm a dork?" Sam asked.

"I'll try my best," she said as Sam moved a little away from her so they could look at each other while they talked. "But if you're going to tell me you still wear your retainer at night to keep those teeth so straight, I won't think you're too much of a dork for that."

"Very funny." Sam laughed anyway, and the tease made her appear more relaxed. "When you came to work for my dad and he first introduced us, I had a serious crush on you from that day on. I didn't think you knew I was alive until you came to my graduation and gave me this string of pearls." Sam opened her collar a little so she could see that she'd worn them. "When I looked down and saw you sitting next to Daddy, I figured he'd twisted your arm to get you there."

"Huey was about to pop a button when you walked across that stage."

Sam shook her head and put her hand up. "I'm not looking for reassurance of how proud my father is of me."

"Think of this part of the conversation as a repeat of your first day of work."

"What do you mean?" Sam asked, tapping their fingers together nervously.

"You didn't let me finish then like you are now, so you're

jumping ahead without reading the report," she said as she tapped the top of Sam's hand.

"You brought homework for me?"

Chili nodded and laughed. "It's back in the car, so pay attention. I was proud of you too, but that's not why I accepted Huey's invitation to your graduation."

"Why'd you go?"

"Because I wanted to share that moment with you." She brushed Sam's hair back unnecessarily but needed the contact. "You have more of an impact on people than you realize, Sam. I've known you're alive for a long time, and I gave you the pearls because I thought they'd make you happy."

"So you're admitting crushes go both ways?"

"Nah. I'd never be dorky enough to admit to a crush," she said with a large smile, and Sam slapped her shoulder though she was laughing. "Okay, maybe a little crush, but Huey's right about one thing, and because I know what he just recently told you—" She stopped because the truth of how unsuccessful she'd been with women would be her ruination going forward.

The real funny thing was she hadn't really ever admitted to herself that she wanted to move ahead one day, so she'd never worried about it. That tomorrow had finally come, and the joke would be on her when Sam or anyone else got the whole truth and thought it wasn't worth taking the chance.

"The day I asked Daddy about Paula he told me he wanted someone better for me."

"I want someone better for you than Paula too. Trust me, she should come with a priest and a gaggle of chanting monks to keep her demons down to a minimum."

"You're hilarious. I meant he warned me about you." Sam laughed and scooted around so they were facing each other and their knees were touching. "The problem with his argument is that you can't choose happiness for someone."

"Why not give Huey the benefit of the doubt? You're right

but *he's* right about me?" She leaned back against the rail and couldn't help steering the conversation in this direction. It was better to face rejection now than when they encountered too many more of the Paulas in her life.

"Are you trying to talk me out of this—whatever this is?" Sam pointed out to the darkness and the picnic basket.

"In truth, after we ran into Paula and how that went, I'm shocked we're here at all."

"You want to hear what's next on my list?" Sam moved again to sit next to her.

"Let me have it." The change of subject wasn't lost on her, but she went along because she wanted that next step. And she wanted it enough to gamble on the hurt that might come of it.

"Your flowers were perfect, I can't believe you found the band, and the picnic was delicious, so thank Dale for me." The lights ahead outlined the city, so their time was almost up. "The next time is up to you."

"Whatever I want?"

"Anything you want that doesn't include nudity or sex, and at the end of that date you can tell me about Sophie Grossman."

She laughed and gazed down at Sam. "You don't want to hear it now? We've got time."

"I don't mind waiting. It'll remind you that I'm not Paula or Sophie, and it'll be cathartic for you to purge all that out of your system," Sam said, and gently pinched the top of her thigh. "But what you have to remember is that I have eighty things on my list."

"I haven't forgotten."

"Let's make a deal then," Sam said as she held her hand out.

"What?" She didn't take Sam's hand yet.

"If you have more than eighty women to tell me about at the end of all those dates, I'm upping my list." Sam extended her hand again. "You're not scaring me off, so deal?"

"Deal," she said as she shook Sam's hand, then kissed her knuckles. When Sam smiled at that, Chili decided to stop worrying and brush up her resume. Huey wouldn't be happy, but all he could do was fire her. She didn't think he had it in him to have her legs broken or worse for having impure thoughts about Sam.

"I promise it won't be boring," Sam said.

"I believe you."

❖

Sam spotted her father a few parking spaces from her the next morning and smiled when he waved. After Chili had dropped her off before midnight and walked her to her door and only kissed the back of her hand, Sam had found three messages from her father, so she was expecting an inquisition. And since he was moving toward her instead of for the door, that was about to begin.

"Good morning, sunshine," Huey said after he opened her door for her. "You feeling okay?"

She lifted both her eyebrows in confusion. "Do I look sick?" She took his arm and walked with him, trying to not to rise to the bait he was throwing out.

"You're as beautiful as ever, but I called you quite a few times last night, and you never answered."

"So your first conclusion was illness? Thank God you're not a cop. With hunches like that you'd have a whole lot of innocent people serving life sentences."

"No. I happened to see Maria and her partner last night, and when I couldn't reach you, I figured that's who you were with. Seeing that you weren't made me worry something was wrong."

"I didn't want to intrude on their evening since they haven't had too much alone time lately, so I stayed home, turned my phones off, and listened to some music. After that it was a quiet night for me." She saw Chili's car in her peripheral vision but kept walking. Her explanation wasn't entirely untrue. The band Chili had hired had played music and their river cruise was pretty quiet. "Did you need something?"

"It wasn't time for our usual dinner night, but I thought you might want to go out and talk. I know it seems like I'm piling on by telling you about Sophie Grossman so soon after you asked about Paula."

She hesitated, wanting to know what her father had to gain by totally discrediting Chili like this, other than to cool her jets when it came to Chili. "Actually, I do want to talk about that, but this isn't the place."

"Want to do lunch?"

"My curiosity can wait, so tomorrow night will be good. We're having lunch with Virgil and his family to go over a few more things. It's crunch time and there's still a lot to do."

"Tomorrow night then."

She got into the elevator with him and waved when Huey continued up to the top floor. A few minutes later Chili hadn't made it up yet, so she texted her.

Where are you?

She laughed like she did every morning when she saw the cubicle Chili's assistant had assigned her. Obviously Paul didn't think of her as a vindictive person, since it was the crummiest one of the bunch. She guessed it was to not show favoritism because of her last name.

I saw your dad so I decided to run away. Maybe I'll find courage after a plate of eggs.

You're full of crap. Sam tapped out her message, glad it was still somewhat quiet.

Or I could be sitting in the cafe down the street ignoring my work duties because I'm planning a date.

"Sam." Paul's voice on the intercom interrupted her fun. "Paula Stern's on line two for you."

"For me? She didn't ask for Chili?"

"No, and once I tell Chili she asked for you, I'm sure she'll give you a raise and a desk that doesn't wobble."

"Thanks," she said as she stared at Chili's last text before moving her gaze to the blinking line on her office phone. "This is Sam, can I help you?"

"Good morning, Sam." Paula paused, then laughed as if anything she said was the pure definition of wit. "I thought we could meet this afternoon for drinks so we can finalize Virgil's campaign."

"We're having lunch with him today and that's on the agenda. Besides, I really don't have the authority to finalize anything." The last thing she wanted was to bond with Paula.

Paula laughed again. "You got me there. Actually, I thought we could get to know each other now that the campaign's almost over. Trust me, I can give you some pointers, especially when it comes to your future employees."

"Future employees?" She wanted to gag and thought of kicking Chili in the butt for ever finding anything remotely attractive about this revolting woman. Granted, she did have a nice ass, but it wasn't nice enough to negate the fact that Paula was the most obnoxious person she'd ever met. "Are you asking me for a job? If you are, for the record, I'm sitting in a cubicle."

"We both know where you'll end up, but that's not what I meant. You seem infatuated with your boss, and no one knows her like I do. I thought you'd appreciate a quick tutorial on what not to do when it comes to the great poll-vaulter."

"Thanks for the offer, but I'm booked up, and I don't like talking about my friends behind their backs."

"Wise up. Once she gets what she's after, she'll find another mountain to conquer. Chili Alexander has no friends."

"Easy climbs usually do lead people to search out new challenges, Ms. Stern. Have a great day, unless you need anything else." The dial tone made her laugh.

"Samantha?" She glanced up at hearing her name, finding the same flower-delivery guy from the night before. "Are you Samantha?" he asked, as if he'd never once laid eyes on her.

If she didn't know the truth, she'd swear she was still dreaming because the day was so bizarre thus far. "Yes, that's me," she said, and he winked.

"Must be your birthday," he said, and turned so she could see the arrangement of orchids. "Or someone really likes you."

"Seems like it. What's your name?"

"Jerry, but my friends call me Daisy."

"Seriously?"

"It's meant with love, but it's caused a few black eyes along the way if you want to get snippy about it." Like he did before, he put the flowers down and made sure they were perfect.

"Thanks, Daisy." She took his hand when he was done. "If you don't mind me calling you that."

"I've got a feeling we'll be good friends, so call me whatever you want," he said softly. "Great meeting you."

She wondered why Daisy had raised his voice, then noticed her father going into Chili's office. "At least I'll have a friend in the floral business when Daddy keels over in a fit and takes Chili with him."

❖

"Who's Sam getting flowers from?" Huey asked as he glanced out the glass wall Chili had insisted on so the staff would feel comfortable coming into the space.

"A Bradford something." She smiled as she listed the precincts for Virgil's campaign on the board.

"You're such an asshole sometimes." When she glanced back at him he was still looking out toward what she assumed was Sam's cubicle. "Has she been getting along with everyone?"

"Sam's fine, but you, I'm not so sure about."

"What are you talking about?" He sat down and crossed his legs.

"When I first met you, Sam was in high school, and back then you didn't act like the guy with a shotgun guarding his girl's virtue. She starts working here and you're beginning to unravel." She finished writing and dropped into her chair. The night with Sam had left her charged enough to be awake for the rest of it after she'd dropped Sam off, so now she was running on caffeine. "Who knew you were this big a nut job?"

"I sign your paychecks."

"No, you don't. Julie from accounting direct-deposits my check, so tell me why you're down here."

"What did you do last night?"

She stared at him until he broke first and lowered his head. "I took Paula Stern and Sophie Grossman home last night and broke out my vat of oil, a roll of Visqueen, and porn tapes. If I were Bacchus I couldn't have thought up that much debauchery, but the company was inspiring."

"Cut the bull." Huey's eyes were glued to his lap. "After our talk, I was surprised when Sam said you took her out last night."

"In my time as a sexually active adult I've done some crazy stuff that's gotten me chased by some daddies along the way, but that hasn't happened since my sophomore year of college." She took a blank sheet of stationery out and started writing. "Some men go bat-shit crazy over their children, and I totally get that.

My dad defends me like that up to a point, but if he was here every day beating you over the head every time someone looked at me funny, I'm sure it'd get old."

"True, but I thought we had a deal." Huey was looking at her now with a somewhat smug expression.

"Sam," she said, and Huey's face went blank when she kept the phone on intercom.

"What can I do for you?"

"Get the staff started on Virgil's briefing for today." The sudden panic disappeared from Huey's expression. "What'd you do last night?" Huey's exhale was long and loud.

"Stayed home and listened to music to try to unwind. Why do you ask? I'm curious because that's been a popular subject today, and if one more person asks me I'm going to have to put out a newsletter."

"Fascinating reading, I'm sure." She picked up the phone and gently put it back down to disconnect from Sam. "There's a meeting with Virgil today," she said as she put her coat back on and shouldered her bag. "And Rooster's expecting a contract by early next week."

"Okay," Huey said, sounding as if he'd just realized something was wrong. "You need my help with anything?"

"Nope." She handed him the sheet of paper she'd folded down the middle. "I just thought you might want to make a list so you won't forget anything."

Everyone stopped talking when she walked to the elevator and punched the button. She never took the elevator, so that must've been the cause for the stillness. This will give me plenty of time to plan all my romantic dates, she thought as she got in and leaned against the back wall of the car.

❖

"Where's Chili going?" Sam asked as she noticed the letter Huey still hadn't opened. "What's that?"

"My to-do list, I guess." Huey finally unfolded the note, and Sam couldn't help but rush to his side when he paled and said, "I've got to go." Huey dropped the sheet and rushed to the elevator and started pressing the button repeatedly.

Until Bradford gets here, I'll take myself out of the picture so you won't have to worry about me. Thanks for everything. You've been a great teacher, but as your friend let me teach you something now. No one needs to tell you what a wonderful woman Sam is, I think you have that part down, but give her the right to find her path. If you don't, the destination will never really be hers. I know you love her, but if you keep pushing her in the direction you think is best, she'll never really be happy.

Again, thank you for all the lessons you taught me along the way. That there'll be no classes saddens me, but please accept my resignation.

"Chili, you're going to pray to die from throwing yourself on your sword and not from me kicking you real hard," Sam said softly when she read the letter for the third time.

She went back to her office for her cell phone, and the second she picked up it rang. "Tell me you aren't serious?" Sam whispered into the phone.

"Don't make waves, and Tsunami Huey will calm down." Sam heard a bunch of car horns and squealing tires. "Idiot," Chili yelled.

"Slow down and tell me why you did this."

"To get what I want shouldn't compromise who I am, and I don't want it to."

Sam closed her eyes and prayed for patience. "Pretend you're not Confucius and explain what you mean."

Chili told her about the talk she'd had with Huey. "So he threw the question out, and had I not grown up with the female version of Elliott Ness, I might've fallen for it. I knew you hadn't told him we went out on a date last night, but I don't want to lie to him either."

"So you want to give up?"

"Sam, breathe, okay?" Chili said, and Sam heard more car horns. "Against reasonable thinking, I resigned my job today after a picnic because I'd like to go out with you again. A part of me thinks it's unreasonable, because from the first day I started working there nothing has ever meant more to me than that job."

"I don't want you to quit." Sam could hear her heartbeat in her ear. "We're not off to an auspicious start, huh?"

"When you're old and start on your memoirs, this will guarantee you have to write about what a wonderful person you thought I was. I want to read the phrase 'goddess-like' more than a couple of times."

"Stop it, this is serious."

Chili laughed and Sam relaxed. "This is going to make me sound like I know how to play people to get what I want, but forget about this morning and have Beth help you run Virgil's meeting today."

"Why would that make you sound bad?"

"Because given a few days of torturing himself for gambling on a bad bet, your father will back down. Once he does, we won't have to lie."

"Just omit the obvious?"

"Tell me what you want," Chili said in a monotone fashion, and Sam wanted to leave the office.

"No sense in scaring you off for good if I'm completely honest. Not that I think you'd get far in that box you drive."

"Scare me later then, and call me after you decipher my note."

"I'm reading your note and I get that you quit."

Chili's laugh was making her fear disappear. "Not that note. The one with the flowers Daisy delivered."

Sam reached for it and read it more than once, wondering what Chili could've meant. "Were you drunk when you wrote this?"

"No hints. You have to figure it out on your own," Chili said, then hung up.

For the rest of the day Sam went through the motions except when they met with Virgil. He was so nice Sam couldn't help but give her all. Her father sat through the meeting but watched the door more than he paid attention. She was guessing he was wishing for the same thing, but Chili didn't appear.

"Have you heard from Chili today?" Huey asked Sam outside Virgil's headquarters.

"She called before we left the office. Where is she?"

"You read the letter, I'm sure, so why ask?"

"Never mind. I'm sure you know what's best, Daddy."

"I'm beginning to wonder about that," Huey said, and didn't complain when she got in the car without inviting him to get in. She'd driven him there but she left alone, sure someone else would take him back to the office. "Okay, what the hell does that note mean?" she asked when Chili answered her phone.

"Are you home yet?"

"The mariachis aren't waiting for me, are they?"

"Could be, but I don't want to ruin the surprise. Before you ask for any more clues, would you have dinner with me tonight?"

"We have a date."

"Good, but right now you've got a date with a man named Daisy."

CHAPTER ELEVEN

Sam studied herself in the full-length mirror attached to her closet door. When she'd gotten home, Daisy had handed over another package, then left laughing. After she opened it and found the antique decoder ring, she joined in. However, a few minutes later, the gibberish on the note became something that made her happy.

She twitched the dress she'd picked one more time when she heard the knock and took a deep breath to settle her nerves. Chili was ten minutes early, according to the clock on her nightstand, and that actually relaxed her more than anything. So far Chili hadn't acted at all like she thought she would, and it was throwing her off a little.

Maria had been right about the number of people interested in dating Sam while she was in college and how picky she'd been. She'd had a good time, but she'd never gotten serious with anyone. The fact that some people could be jerks after a few dates made her shiver to think what they'd be like if she'd given them a real chance and lowered her defenses.

"You're beautiful," Chili said when she opened the door.

"Thank you," Sam answered, and her phone started ringing. "Do you want to come in?"

"Do you want to let Huey know where we're going?" Chili pointed to the phone as she stepped in.

"I think he needs to sweat it out, don't you?"

Chili had on a greatcoat, and her shoes appeared to be made of nice Italian leather. She didn't seem obsessive about it, but Chili always looked well put together, which made her wonder who'd taught Chili all that style.

"I love your father so I don't like seeing him in pain."

"Even if it's of his own making?" She picked up her coat and smiled when Chili took it from her.

"Huey loves you, so don't give him too hard a time." Chili helped her on with her coat, then rested her hands on Sam's shoulders. "You ready?"

Having Chili this close made her turn around and put her arms around Chili's waist. "Would you do something for me before we go?"

"Sure." Chili lifted her hand and cupped Sam's cheek. "What?"

"Kiss me." Sam needed to know how big the spark between them was.

Chili lowered her head and stopped right before she reached her lips. So far this exceeded anything Sam had ever fantasized about, and then Chili kissed her. She pressed her lips to Sam's, and Sam could've sworn every cell in her body came alive and electrified. No way in hell was she was giving this up for anything, if a kiss caused this reaction. The sex, she figured, would send her into an altered state.

"Wow," Sam said when their lips parted.

Chili opened her eyes and kissed her one more time. "Wow is right." After that, Chili stepped back as if she couldn't behave if they stayed that close. "Thanks. I was going to try to figure out over dinner how to get you to kiss me. Who knew coming out and asking was the way to go."

"Why?" Sam asked, as she followed Chili when she moved.

"Sometimes your heart—"

"Doesn't live up to the hype," Sam said, taking a chance she was right.

"Precisely." Chili took her hand. "You never gave me the impression you were interested in me, but I'm glad you are."

"That doesn't sound very romantic."

"True, but romance has never been a huge part of my life up to now." Chili picked her purse up and handed it to her so they could leave.

"You're more of a hunter-gatherer, huh?"

"More like a hunter-borrower since I didn't want to keep anything I gathered. Politics isn't a romance kind of thing, especially the politics of today." Chili opened the car door for her and helped her put her seat belt on.

The stiffness in Chili's movements made Sam smile. Chili was the best at her job, but when it came to anything like this, she was definitely a novice. What had she said at her parents' anniversary party? Chili's parents were the best role models when it came to love, and she'd never thought she'd find the same thing, so Chili had obviously neglected this part of her life.

"If I tell you something, will you do the same?"

"How about if I go first?" Chili got in and turned to face her before starting the car. "You're a beautiful woman, Sam, and when I was at your graduation I kept thinking about one thing. If I'm honest, it was something I thought when you worked with us during your breaks."

Sam took one of Chili's hands between hers. "You can tell me."

"I thought about how I'd work with you every day and not become someone you'd eventually take out a restraining order on. On your first day I had to laugh at myself for not seeing the truth sooner."

"Let me in on the joke."

"You're my first crush, and I wasn't sure how to handle the

truth of it. Considering how your first day ended, I didn't think I'd have to worry about it for too long." Chili laughed and shook her head. "Then you told me about your list, and I realized I couldn't research it to come up with a plan. It's just something to do because I want to."

"You've got a crush on me?"

"I know, dorky, huh?"

Sam shook her head and leaned forward. "No, it's nice to know it's a fair playing field." Chili started the car and headed to the interstate but didn't let Sam's hand go. "We're going out of town?" Sam asked.

"You can get mad at me now, but no. I thought about you and what you'd consider romantic. A short trip to the boonies didn't strike me as that."

"You're hilarious." Chili took the exit that led to the lake, but Sam wasn't familiar with any restaurants in the area. "Another picnic?"

"Before you freak out on me, we're having dinner at my place. I wanted to be alone with you, and Dale taught me how to cook something to impress you."

Chili had been gone all day, and knowing she was with Dale learning how to cook for her was incredibly sexy. "You cooking for me isn't going to freak me out."

"Dale told me this dish is better cooked with no barriers between me and the stove, which I took to mean I had to make it naked, so I'm glad you're so open-minded." Chili drove over the levee, then stopped and came around to open her door again.

"As enticing as that sounds, how about you keep your clothes on this time around so we don't have to rush to the emergency room later when you literally burn your ass? That'll put a crimp in my plans if I get frisky later." They held hands on the walk to the end of the pier, and Sam was anticipating what Chili's house would be like. "This is your place?"

"It's nice to come home to." Chili unlocked her door and

waved her inside. "It's the one location I could find that allows me to decompress from the bullshit we have to put up with sometimes."

"Have you ever shared it with anyone?" It was a petty question, but she was still in the research phase of this operation.

"Your dad's been out a few times, and Dale comes once a week to cook for me, but he's not interested in me romantically. If you're talking about women, there's no way I'd give up the location. Since up to now all those hookups have ended not so great, why would I give them somewhere to start giving me shit day and night? When it comes to this place, you're the first."

After they went in, Chili handed her a glass of wine and went into the kitchen to start dinner. Chili hadn't put any more moves on her after their couple of kisses, and Sam was sure if she did have another seventy-eight things on a list in her head, Chili would give her what she wanted. She was shocked she'd found the mariachi band, but this wasn't about torturing Chili. If she needed any convincing about the depth of Chili's honor, it'd come when she'd resigned earlier.

"That deserves a reward."

❖

Dale had written the instructions so that a three-year-old could finish the dish he'd come up with and had demonstrated at lunch. Chili would've called and insulted him if she hadn't wanted to make a good impression. The oven timer went off so she took out the starters Dale had made, saying hors d'oeuvres were a completely different lesson, and considering her total lack of skills in the kitchen, she didn't have time to learn, so he'd made them. She took out the mushroom cheese puffs and placed them on the tray Dale had given her, the way he'd told her to do it.

She slid the chicken into the oven and took a deep breath

before heading to the other room. It was ridiculous, but she was nervous. "How about one of these." She walked into the den and held the tray out, then promptly dropped it.

Sam was sitting on the sofa with her arms resting on the back with her legs crossed. None of that would've been strange had it not been for the fact that she was naked, completely naked. "Ah, Sam."

"Do you think we can talk a little before dinner?" Sam uncrossed her legs and leaned forward enough for Chili to forget how to breathe. "Come sit down."

She moved forward like she was on an incline and was having trouble keeping her balance. When she was close to the sofa, Sam stood up and ran her hands down her right arm until she reached the cuff of her shirt. Sam unbuttoned that first before moving to the other one, and then she unbuttoned the shirt until she reached the waist of her pants.

"On the chance of sounding like an idiot, what are you doing?" Chili asked as Sam pulled on the sides of her shirt to get it out of her pants.

"I thought your brother said cooking naked would make the food taste better," Sam said as she worked on the buttons as they appeared. "I didn't want you to be shy about it."

Sam lowered the shirt from her shoulders and let it drop to the floor. "Are you sure about this?" she asked, hoping the answer wouldn't be no.

Sam unbuckled her belt and unbuttoned her pants, letting them fall to her ankles before she said, "Are you going to forget who I am tomorrow morning?"

"No." She had chills when Sam hooked her fingers into the sides of her underwear and followed them down.

"Then sit."

That Sam had so effectively taken over like this was turning her on. It was certainly different than any other time she'd been with a woman, but if Sam wanted to seduce her, it wouldn't be hard. What she didn't want was regret if they moved too fast. "Should I remind you that we've got quite a few more dates to go?"

"I expect you to come through," Sam said as she knelt between her legs, gently running her fingertips down her thighs to her knees and back up.

Before she could think of any other objections, Sam spread her open and ran her tongue from the opening of her sex to the bottom of her clitoris. Finding Sam naked had made her wet, but this got her instantly ready and desperate for an orgasm. Sam, though, obviously had other plans, since she slowed her movements and sucked her in softly. At this rate she'd rattle apart.

Chili sat back and enjoyed the slow burn, then opened her eyes when Sam moved to straddle her. If this was a dream, she hadn't had one this good since she was fifteen and had discovered reruns of *Wonder Woman*. Sam smiled down at her and her nipples got rock hard. She hoped Sam wasn't going to change her mind as she put her hands under Sam's ass and pulled her closer. When Sam kissed her she stood up and walked to the corner of the room, where the spiral stairs led to the master bedroom upstairs.

She laid Sam down and took her socks off before joining her. "Would you believe I'm nervous?" she asked as she rested her hand on the curve of Sam's hip.

"Do you know how long I've waited to be in this position?" Sam reached down and grabbed her hand. "Let me try to relax you," she said as she dragged Chili's hand up and placed it around her breast. "Does this loosen you up any?"

If Chili went through with this, it meant commitment. She couldn't go back to the life she knew if she hurt Sam, and she wouldn't want to. With a slight nod she moved so she was covering Sam with her body and encouraged Sam to spread her legs. She lowered her head and kissed Sam.

She wanted to go slow, but having Sam under her like this put her hunger into overdrive. It was like putting an ice-cream sundae with all the trimmings in front of a three-year-old and expecting the kid not to take a bite. When Sam arched up into her, she knew she'd never possess that kind of willpower with this woman.

After another kiss, Chili lowered her head and ran the tip of her tongue around Sam's pink, puckering nipple. Sam raked her nails up her back when she sucked it in, and it made her want more. She reached down and put her hand between Sam's legs. With one stroke she knew Sam was ready.

"Please, baby," Sam said as she grabbed her butt and pressed her closer.

Chili rested her weight on her elbow so she could reach. Sam's wetness and hard clitoris made her want to linger so she stroked slowly, drenching her fingers. She'd never wanted to please someone like she did Sam, so she took two fingers and slid them in, making Sam release a long, satisfied-sounding moan.

When Sam opened up to her she went down Sam's body until she could taste her. It was like Sam was hypersensitive, so when she put her mouth on her, Sam bucked up and grabbed both sides of Chili's head and pressed her tighter against her. From the movements of Sam's hips to the moans that were coming at faster intervals, Chili knew she didn't have much time, so she sucked the hard clit into her mouth and slammed her fingers in and kept them there. Sam's back came completely off the bed, and she called out her name before slumping back down.

Chili moved up again and took Sam into her arms, and it was then that she noticed Sam was crying. She wasn't hysterical, but large fat tears were making their way down her face, and the sight of them broke Chili's heart. A moment of paradise wasn't worth losing a friend and everything that could've come of it, the job be damned. Sam was much more important than that.

"I'm so sorry, Sam," she said as she rubbed her back. "It'll be okay, I promise."

"You don't have to apologize," Sam said as she wiped her face with the sheet. "This has never happened to me, but you kind of overwhelmed me."

"As long as you're not crying because it sucked," she joked, trying to get Sam to smile.

"I happen to like the way you suck, so don't worry about it, and you definitely live up to the hype." Sam took a deep breath and moved so she was lying on top. "And now I'd love to finish what we started in the other room."

Before Chili could respond, Sam moved down and spread her legs and moved them so they were bent at the knee. "Are you sure?" She didn't want to push Sam if the tears weren't connected to a short circuit of her emotions.

"Am I sure I want to do this?" Sam asked as she put her tongue at the base of her clit. She flattened her tongue and moved it up until she got to the top, and then she started flicking her tongue until Chili cursed. "The real question is if you want me to stop?"

"Right now I'll pay you not to," Chili said, and Sam laughed.

"You don't strike me as the kind of person who pays for sex, but I'll sell Fudge the exclusive if you do," Sam said before she went back to what she was doing. It took less than two minutes for Sam to drive her completely insane.

No matter how much she moved, Sam kept pace, and when she couldn't hold the orgasm back any longer, Chili thought she'd break out in tears. It was so good she thought she heard bells, which had never happened. Then she had to laugh when she realized it was the oven timer going off. Her roasted chicken was done.

"What's so funny?" Sam asked as she moved so she was covering her body again.

"I heard that bell and thought you'd gotten your orgasm wings." Sam laughed before she leaned down and kissed her.

"Now that the appetizer part of our evening is over, are you hungry?"

"Starving, but I'm interested in another picnic."

"Let me grab your clothes and I'll be right back. Where do you want to eat?"

Sam ignored her and walked to the closet, where she took a shirt off its hanger and put it on. "We're not going anywhere, so put on a robe if you own one."

They walked downstairs together, and Chili hoped she wasn't going to have any other visitors for the rest of the night. The pile of clothes in the den would be hard to explain. "The night isn't going like I planned, so don't blame me if the chicken is dry."

Sam laughed as she pulled the tie to her robe. "You're complaining?"

"Read between the lines, cute stuff. I'm asking you on another date if dinner isn't perfect." She closed the robe and took the chicken out and cut it into some easy-to-handle pieces and placed them on a small platter.

"That smells good. Do you need any help?"

Chili grabbed two napkins and the platter and pointed to the den. "I don't think I'm coordinated enough to make the sides I had in mind, so all you need to do is sit and eat some chicken."

"Are you upset the night is going like this?" Sam asked as she grabbed the bottle of wine Chili had taken out of the refrigerator and the two glasses on the counter.

"That's not a serious question, is it?" She put the food down and sat on the floor next to the coffee table. Sam accepted the hand she held out and sat on her lap. "Are you worried about anything?"

"I don't want you to think I'm rushing you."

"If anyone who knew me well heard you say that, they'd die laughing."

"Paula wants to take me out for drinks to warn me about the

big hungry wolf," Sam said, making her laugh. "This is the first time we've done this, but I know you. I'm not worried."

"I'm not going to propose tomorrow," she said, and Sam lost her smile. "But I am going to be here tomorrow. I'm not going anywhere, Sam."

"That's all I need to hear. Looking too far into the future is sometimes scary, but if you take it a day at a time, I promise to put you at ease." Sam picked up a piece of chicken and fed it to her as she took some bites of her own. "Speaking of tomorrow, what are you going to do about getting your job back?" Sam asked.

"Your dad has to come around. If he doesn't, then I'll have to think about it. I don't want to go to work for the competition, but I'm too young to retire."

"Do you want me to do anything?"

"No. Huey's a big boy, and it has to be his decision. I can always help Rooster win and run his office here after he ships off to Washington."

"You'd be bored out of your mind in a week."

She laughed before taking a sip of wine. "I'll be seeing you, so I doubt that."

"You'll be doing much more than that with me."

She kissed Sam and encouraged her to turn and face her. "Maybe I should go work with Rooster, since it's going to be hard to not give away my feelings when you look at me like this."

"What are your feelings?" Sam opened her robe, then started unbuttoning the shirt she'd thrown on.

"In general or right now?"

Sam smiled as she took Chili's hand and lifted it so she could put one of her fingers in her mouth. "Right now, and that's all I want you to concentrate on," Sam said as she took two of Chili's fingers in to the knuckles. "Like I said, if that's all we both do, I'm sure that a whole bunch of days will go by and you won't be able to live without me."

Chili put her hand in the center of Sam's chest and pushed

her back a little so she could reach one of her nipples. It puckered stone hard in her mouth, and Sam threaded her hand into the hair at the back of her head. Before she could move to the other breast, Sam took the hand that she'd sucked the fingers on and positioned it so she could mount them. Sam was wet again, and she held her breast up to her like a gift.

As Chili looked at her, that's exactly what Sam was to her. Finally fate had sent her a present that it would kill her to return.

"That I already know," she said as she laid Sam down and started her quest to make Sam hers.

❖

"Are you sure about my father?" Sam asked after they'd dressed and were walking back to Chili's car. "One of the best parts of my job is working with you."

"I'm not giving in, so we'll have to wait him out. If he doesn't come around in a week, I promise I'll talk to him." Chili opened her door and Sam watched her walk around the front of her car. She was definitely moving slower now than when Chili had picked her up. "I should've told you to pack a bag so it doesn't seem like I'm kicking you out after a great night."

"Waking up with you would've been a good way to start tomorrow, but I don't want you to think I'm packing the U-Haul and picking china patterns." She leaned over the console so she could rest her head on Chili's shoulder.

"I could always surprise you and pack you up myself."

The comment came close to making her lift her head to see if Chili was joking, because it didn't sound like it. They drove in comfortable silence after that, and even though she told Chili to go on, she walked her to her door again.

"Thanks for dinner and for the best date I've been on," she said as she held Chili's hands.

"Are you busy tomorrow?" Chili was propped against the door frame smiling at her.

"Unless it's work-related, let's go with I'm not busy in the future. I'm all yours if you have something in mind."

"I'll think of something." After that Chili kissed her for a few minutes, as if trying to convey how much she'd miss her until they saw each other again.

She closed the door and rested against it, suddenly cold. It was way too early, but Chili was weaving herself into her soul to the point that she was empty now that she was alone again. When the phone rang she starting laughing but decided to answer it even if it was probably her father. If it was, she could start to speed up his thought process when it came to Chili.

"Hello," she said, trying to project joy into her voice.

"Were you out having sex?"

"Am I supposed to report back to you if I have," she asked Maria as she kicked off her shoes and headed to her bedroom. It was late but she wasn't sleepy, and having shared a shower with Chili she didn't have anything else to do but go to bed, so she was glad for the distraction.

"Never mind. Your answer gives you away." Maria laughed and waited for her to say something, but the reporter part of her friend was going to have to work harder than that for a serious answer.

"No, it doesn't, so don't put words in my mouth. Why are you calling me after midnight anyway?" She unzipped her dress and had a craving for Chili to be pressed up against her. The skin-on-skin contact had been her definition of nirvana.

"The jungle drums are beating loudly tonight, so I was calling you to confirm my story."

"Did I miss a class in school that would've clued me in to all the cryptic talk? What story?" She pulled out her oldest but most comfortable flannel nightgown and tossed it on.

"Word on the street, sweetie, is that Chili quit and is being courted by at least three firms and two major campaigns. What the hell happened?"

She took the phone from her ear and stared at it for a minute. "Can I call you right back?"

"You promise you'll give me a statement, and you can call me whenever you want."

Chili was probably still on the road so she dialed her number, having already memorized it. "Reporters are calling my house wanting the Chili scoop," she said when Chili answered.

"What's the bullshit going around? Am I running the presidential race for the idiot from Alaska, or have I been downgraded to traffic-court elections?" Chili laughed, and Sam could hear the radio in the background. "Maria must be desperate for a story if she's calling about that at this hour."

"I didn't say it was Maria."

"It wasn't?" Chili shot back with a little heat. "Sorry. I just think she's a little too familiar with you, partner or no."

"No need for jealousy, babe. Maria was my first roommate in college, and after a few dates we figured we were better off as friends since we had about as much spark as two wet matches in a hurricane. And to answer your question, that *is* who called me, and you know her well enough that she's not going to quit until I tell her something." She got into bed and sighed, since it was three times bigger than the night before. "You didn't tell me you've gotten so many offers, none of which have anything to do with traffic court."

"That's Maria's way of fishing for a story. She throws a box of dynamite in the water and sees what floats up once she's killed everything in the lake."

"She wants me to call her back and give her a statement about what happened. What do you want me to tell her?" She rolled to her side and stared at the empty pillow next to her, imagining Chili being there.

"Call your dad and ask him. I'd tell you what to say, Sam, but it's Huey's firm, and he should have final say when it comes to any media inquiries."

"If I ask you to do something for me, would you?" In the quiet of the town house it was easy to hear the tapping, as if something was hitting her window. She flew out of her bed and laughed when she saw Chili standing on the sidewalk with another handful of acorns.

"Hopefully your question had something to do with asking me back up?" Chili asked as she held her phone to her ear.

"You could work the Quarter with psychic instincts like that." She practically skipped back to the front door and stood waiting until Chili showed up. "I know you didn't make it home to pack that bag you were talking about, but you're not leaving until the morning."

"Don't worry about that." Chili hung up and picked her up and carried her in the direction she pointed to. She threw the phone on the bed as she worked to get Chili undressed. "Before we get too involved and you get visitors in the morning because of it, call your father."

"Right now?" She stripped her nightgown off and straddled Chili when she lay down.

"Get him to feed you some lines, since Maria wants an answer. Trust me, he won't freak out. No matter what time I call him he's always awake, or at least he sounds incredibly alert, which makes me think he has vampiric tendencies, but everyone has their little secrets."

"What do you think my secret is?" she asked as she took the phone from Chili.

"You're multi-orgasmic, but that's not a secret anymore. That's more like our little secret now, and I'll take it to my grave." When Chili said it, she got wet and hoped Chili wouldn't mind another shower after she painted her abdomen from top to bottom later.

"What else?" she asked as she pressed her center down to get some relief.

"You're excellent under pressure," Chili said, pointing to the phone, then moved her hand down Sam's body until it was between her legs.

"You're not that cruel, are you?" She dropped the phone when Chili stroked her need back to life with a vengeance.

"There'll never be any cruelty between us," Chili said as she kept her fingers moving and Sam grabbed her wrist. "And I'll never get enough of you. I don't care who knows because I'm not going anywhere, no matter who doesn't like it." Sam moved up so she could place Chili's fingers where she most needed them and cried out when she came down on them.

She hoped the walls of her apartment were thick enough not to bother her neighbors, but she couldn't hold down the volume when she said Chili's name as she went at her pace until the walls of her sex clamped down on Chili's fingers. Giving in to what she wanted had left her with no regret and a need to be with Chili like this.

Chili lifted her upper body and flipped them so she was on top, but Sam didn't complain since Chili could move her hand better and her strokes were deep and strong. Sam hung on and rested her feet on the back of Chili's thighs, wanting to make it easier to move at the pace Chili had set. It didn't take long for her to surrender and come so hard she started crying again.

"What the hell are you doing to me?" she asked when Chili dropped next to her and held her.

"Something good, I hope," Chili said as she kissed her forehead. "Or maybe I want to get you hooked so you can't live without me."

That answer surprised her more than anything else Chili had said so far that night, and the chill left her body. Maybe loving Chili wasn't such a scary notion, if in turn Chili fell in love with her. Frightening things weren't so bad if you had someone to hold your hand while you worked out the kinks. The prospect that Chili would be next to her made her anticipate what came next, because if Chili's mom was right, it'd be a joyful and color-filled life.

"I might already be there, so don't say things you don't mean," she said, pushing her luck.

"I rarely do," Chili said as the phone rang.

Sam looked at the evil device that had interrupted the most important conversation of her life, but she answered it, not wanting anyone else to show up on her doorstep. When she gazed up at Chili, her smile reassured her that their talk wasn't over. "Hello," she said, putting her head down on Chili's shoulder.

"Sam, did you give Maria Poplin a comment about Chili?" Huey asked, and that it was him saved her a call later.

"No. I told her I'd call her back. I wanted to talk to you first, but I thought it'd be rude to phone you this late," she said, making Chili laugh quietly but enough to shake the bed.

"Have you talked to Chili?" Huey asked, obviously either missing her jibe or choosing to ignore it.

"Daddy, whatever happened between you and Chili is between you and Chili, but if Maria's right, you've got a small window of time to fix it. I doubt Chili is out actively seeking new employment, but once this gossip, which people think it to be now, is confirmed by someone like Maria, it'll be too late. From what you've said about Chili through the years, she won't be available long, and you'll have no one to blame but your pride." Chili moved the hand she had on Sam's stomach and pinched her nipple. She grabbed it before Chili got any other ideas while she was talking to her father.

"I didn't fire her, so don't blame me for this. It was her decision."

Her father seldom sounded like a petulant child but he was

doing a good job of it, and it was starting to work her patience. "Okay, like I said, it's your company, so if Maria wants a comment, call her back and give her one."

"No need to throw me under the bus. I need you to be on my side on this, Sam."

"Okay, tell me who Bradford is, and I'll be happy to do whatever you want me to," she said, and Chili laughed again.

"That's not important," Huey said, extremely too fast and too defensively.

"Then good luck, Daddy." She moved her head to the side so Chili could continue her line of kisses from her shoulder. "Let me know how it turns out tomorrow."

"Wait," Huey said loudly. She figured it was to keep her on the line in case she planned to hang up on him. "If I promise to phone Chili in the morning, will you call Maria back and get her off the scent?"

"It depends."

"On what?" Huey sounded aggravated now.

"Are you calling her to tell her what she wants to hear, or are you going to apologize?" Chili pinched her nipple again, and she reached down and grabbed her hand so she could bite her index finger.

"If it's that important to you I'll apologize."

"Good night, and let's hang up while you think you're ahead," she said, and laughed.

"You get more like your mother every day."

"I'll take that as a compliment." She hung up. "Let me call Maria, and then you get to tell me who Bradford is."

"There's no fun in me telling you, so I'll save that one for your father." Chili rolled them over so she was pressed up against Sam's back. The move gave her full access to the front of Sam's body. "What are you going to tell Maria?"

"That you're not going anywhere since I've stuck my flag of possession in your ass and will shoot anyone who tries to steal you away," she joked as she dialed. "Maria, did you call my father after I hung up?"

"No. I called him before I called you, and since he gave me nothing, I thought I'd get you to spill the coffee if I caught you in one of your dead sleeps."

"So the sex question was to throw me off?" Chili moved her head closer to hear the other side of the conversation.

"I called a bunch of times and you weren't home, so I was hoping that's what you were doing. Were you?"

"I'm not telling you on the chance you're going to add it to the story you're working on, and for your information, Chili's not going anywhere."

"Are you sure? My source said the meeting at Virgil's was missing Chili, and she walked out early this morning. When I heard Huey had gone to the meeting instead, I knew they weren't full of shit and there was something to this. He's your father and I know you love him, but Huey seldom ventures out of that ivory tower, and he doesn't have to because Chili runs the show."

"All I can tell you is what I know, Maria, so don't think I'm trying to be an asshole by putting you off. You can call tomorrow afternoon and ask for Chili. I'm sure she'll give you a quote herself."

"Where were you earlier tonight? That's off the record."

She moved around so she could look at Chili when she answered. "I was out on a date, but I heard you were too, so we're even."

"Not remotely close since you know who my date was. Who were you with?"

"I'd wait to pass you a note in math class tomorrow, but I know you won't leave me alone until I tell you. Chili asked me out and I accepted. A good time was had by all." She smiled at Chili as she reached over and pressed her hand to Chili's cheek.

"Where'd she take you?"

Sam sighed and rolled her eyes. Maria was seldom this

chatty, but when she was it was impossible to get her off the phone. "It's kind of late so can we talk tomorrow?"

"Since when did you become a farmer who needs twelve hours of sleep?"

Chili held her hand up and pointed to the phone, so she handed it over. "Hello, Maria," Chili said, causing momentary silence on the other end. "How about you, Sam, and I go out to lunch tomorrow and we'll answer all the questions you have, up to a point, and all of them are confidential?"

"Out past your curfew, aren't you?" Maria asked, and laughed. "I'll leave you and Sam alone and take you up on your invitation. You can confirm your employment tomorrow, and I am reporting that no matter what you threaten me with."

"I can't wait," Chili said, and hung up. "Sorry if I overstepped there, but sometimes I find she talks in circles to confuse you. We have better ways to spend time."

"As long as you know you just painted a bull's-eye on yourself by talking to her."

"That would worry me if I was afraid of what Maria would find out. If it's that I want to spend time with you and get you to do that as often as I can talk you into it, I don't have a problem." Chili kissed her and encouraged her to roll over again. "You were right about one thing. It's late so let's get some sleep. You want me to go?"

"That's a wasted question. Go to sleep, and don't think of sneaking out on me in the morning."

"You should be thinking about how to get rid of me," Chili said, and put her arm around her waist.

"We shouldn't have too many problems then."

"We'll compare our list of demands soon enough." Chili kissed her on the temple. "Once you find out some of my bad habits you might kick my ass out the door."

"Do you plan to run around with strange women and drink

yourself to sleep every night?" Sam pulled on her finger to get Chili's attention.

"Only on my birthday, and only if you agree to act a little strange for me."

"Good answer."

"I aim to please, and I promise to do my best since you seem to come with a posse that expects perfection."

CHAPTER TWELVE

A re you sure I can't call in sick today?" Sam asked the next morning as they shared a shower. "Your morning workout isn't something I'm about to forget all day. It'll be cruel to make me wait until this afternoon to see you."

Chili turned Sam around and put shampoo in her hair. This was so far out of her usual comfort zone it was crazy, but she couldn't imagine being anywhere but here. "I'm hoping to be back at work today, and if that's the case you have to be there."

"What's on tap for today then? I don't want to be stuck at the office until late tonight."

"You need to talk to Beth this morning and see if she got someone into our opponent's town hall meeting and if he answered the abortion question the way I think he would, given the chance in his backyard with an audience he was comfortable with. I want all of you to meet this morning and work up some mailers and cull the labels to pinpoint the areas where they'll make the most impact." She put Sam under the spray and moved to the conditioner next. "We'll need some volunteers as well to follow up with some personal visits to drive the importance of voting home."

"Is Beth going to wonder where I'm getting all these wonderful orders?"

"Tell her it's in your blood. Don't worry. She'll be fine with taking directions from you."

When they were done, Chili put her pants back on and only the shirt from the night before. It was cold outside, but she figured she could make it to the car without freezing to death.

"Stay out of trouble and answer your phone if my father calls you," Sam said as she walked out of her closet, zipping up her skirt.

"Yes, ma'am."

She got Sam down to her car and walked around the block to pick up hers and get home and change so she could give Huey a call. As she drove up to her spot at home, Huey was already waiting for her, and she was glad she'd taken the time to wash off every essence of Sam.

"Good morning," she said as she held her hand out.

Huey shook it and looked her up and down. "Late night?"

"Could be early morning, but you don't have to worry about me anymore. I did, after all, give you what you wanted." She knew she'd promised Sam, but Huey had forgotten every bit of loyalty she'd given him in the years she'd been with him, so she figured she was due some snippiness.

"I didn't come to preach, Chili. If you want me to beg I will, but can we simply agree to tear up that smart-ass letter you wrote and move on?" He took what looked to be the letter she'd given him and held it up.

"Give me a chance to change and I'll see you at the office." She walked past him and slapped him on the back.

"From now on," Huey said, and then seemed to lose his train of thought when he fell silent.

"We'll be fine, Huey, as long as we go back to that mutual-respect thing we had going. I've never given you a reason to question me, and I'm not planning to, so get going before I write you another note, and this one won't be so nice."

She shook her head when he took a deep breath but then just turned and did as she asked. That was one thing out of the way, so now she could concentrate on more important issues. "Like how to wipe that image of Sam in those pink bikini underwear she was prancing around in this morning from my memory," she said aloud.

Her phone rang as she kicked her shoes off in her bedroom, and Dale's smiling face showed up on the screen. "Did the chicken make an impression?" he asked.

"Will you bug me all day if I say I have no comment?"

"No, since that means I'll be getting a new sister-in-law," he said, and she heard clapping.

"It's a wonder you cook such good stuff, the way you rush things. We had a nice evening and that's all I'm confessing to, besides the fact that *my* chicken dish was a success."

"What about the stir-fried snap peas I put in the fridge?"

"I'm sure those are wonderful too, but I didn't get that far."

"Who knew vegetables were such a challenge and your downfall? Are we still on for tonight?" Dale said, thankfully changing the subject.

Usually kissing and telling wasn't a problem, since she wasn't planning any more than that, but with Sam as the subject it'd be disrespectful. "Do you mind if Sam tags along? I promised dinner tonight, and if you're cooking I'm sure it'll be more well-balanced anyway."

"Not a problem, and I doubt she had any complaints last night. Any requests?"

"Surprise me," she said as she threw a new suit on the bed. "And I love you but I've got to run. I'm already late for work."

"He gave in, huh?"

"For a little while anyway. Once he figures out I'm dating Sam I'm sure he'll chase me through town with his car and murderous thoughts, but I'm dating Sam."

"Good for you, and good for you. I think Sam is exactly what you need in your life."

"For once we agree on something."

❖

"Good morning, Daddy," Sam said when she went up to her father's office at his request. "What can I do for you?"

"I went by Chili's place this morning and we buried the hatchet. She should be here in a little while."

"Since I don't see any blood on you I'm guessing it went okay, and I'm happy for you. I'm not blind as to what Chili means to this place."

Huey nodded and cocked his chair back. "If only she'd grow up and live her life as well as she does this job."

"What's that supposed to mean?"

"She was just getting in when I got there this morning. All that catting around catches up to a person sooner or later, and I keep telling you about her behavior so you don't fall victim to that charm of hers."

Sam tried her best to scowl at his latest attempt to whip up her contempt. "I'm not that easy to sway," she said softly. "And I know bullshit when it's put under my nose, so don't worry about me and what I might fall for." She turned when she reached the door and pointed her finger at him. "I'm not sure where you got the idea that I'm some sort of simpleton when it comes to fast women, but that's not the case. I've met people like Chili Alexander over and over again since I've started dating, and I didn't fall for their crap then. I'm not about to start now and make a fool of myself at work."

"I know that, honey, but I also don't want you to think I'm falling down on the job as your dad." Huey opened his appointment book and flipped to what appeared to be today's date. "What time is the staff meeting downstairs? I might come down and get my feet wet like I did yesterday."

"Beth said in about an hour, but I'll have someone call up for you."

"You want me to pick you up for dinner tonight?"

"Sure," she said, and almost slapped the side of her head since she'd forgotten what was basically a weekly date.

She decided to take the stairs for the two flights down and congratulated herself when she heard footsteps below her. The only person in the office who ever took the stairs was Chili, so she waited on the landing for her to make it up.

"Did you insert a LoJack in my ass cheek when I fell asleep?" Chili said as she pressed Sam to the doorway.

"Clean living and luck made me take the stairs, so I'm not stalking you." Sam put her arms around Chili's waist and turned her face up for a kiss.

"Did you get called to the principal's office then?" Chili didn't hesitate to kiss her and to put her hand on her ass. "It sounded like you were on your way down."

"Daddy wanted to tell me you were back and that he caught you skulking back home in some sort of walk of shame. I hope the woman was worth it." She pinched Chili's side and laughed. "She wasn't some slut you're seeing on the side, was she?"

"I'd never kiss and tell, and that's exactly what I told my brother earlier when he called. Do you mind if he comes over and cooks for us tonight? We get together every week and I don't want to put him off, but I will if you've got other plans."

"Actually Daddy reminded me that tonight is our weekly dinner night."

"I'd invite you both over since Dale loves a crowd, but that'd go over like a dish of raw chicken. One night won't kill us, I guess. It might even make the heart grow fonder, like they say."

"I'm pretty fond of you already, but I'm bummed I won't

get to see you tonight. You could always come over when you're done with Dale." Sam moved her hands up so she could put them behind Chili's neck. "Unless you need the night off."

"Do you fish?"

Strange change of subject, but Chili didn't seem upset or setting her up for anything. "I haven't in years. The only time I remember doing that was when I was little and Daddy took me to some rodeo he was involved with."

"Dale and I go every year. Since he cooks for me I treat him to a couple of trips, and that's what he always picks. One of them is coming up, and if you don't get seasick I thought you might want to come so you two can get to know each other."

"I don't want to intrude," she said, and held her breath when Chili lifted her up a little so she could put her knee between her legs.

"Let's talk about it tonight." Chili kissed her again and let her go, thankfully before she begged to be touched in a way that wasn't appropriate for where they were.

They walked in together and no one looked up or seemed surprised, so Sam followed Chili into her office and sat in the seat closest to her desk. "Daddy wants to come down for the staff meeting."

"Good. I miss him every so often when he's in his hermit moods."

"You really do like him, don't you?" Sam crossed her legs and let her shoe drop off, enjoying Chili's expression.

"I really do, and if you don't want him to know how much I like you, put your shoes back on."

Sam laughed and left Chili to prepare. Paul went in after her and she saw him taking plenty of notes, so she figured it'd be a busy day to make up for the lost time from the day before. When the meeting started she sat next to her father and made a list of everything Chili needed done. It'd be a late night, especially if she had to have dinner with her father.

By the time they finished, it was almost noon, and Sam wondered if Chili was trying to avoid lunch with Maria. "Get going, and don't skip getting something to eat. Since Virgil's counting on us to get all this done we'll be here a while tonight, so call home and make your excuses. If you want, you can blame the bitch you work for," Chili said, making everyone laugh.

Sam's phone pinged with a message from Maria, and from what she read she was already on her way to lunch at one of her favorite locations. "Problem?" Huey asked.

"Maria wants to have lunch so she can get her quote about Chili leaving for bigger and better things."

"Chili, you got plans for lunch?" Huey asked.

"I was going by Dale's since I'll be working late tonight. Why? You trying to wrangle an invitation?" Chili put her coat back on and appeared ready to go.

"No, but Maria called last night about you leaving the firm and wouldn't let it go, so she's expecting a statement from Sam at lunch. Tag along and make sure she knows you're not going anywhere. We don't need this kind of rumor right before some of these major races are deciding which firm to hire."

"I'm sure you and Sam can handle it," Chili said, and Sam scrunched her forehead in confusion over the answer. Her father was giving them the go-ahead to have lunch together, and Chili was trying to talk him out of it.

"I'm sure we could, but it would look like we're trying to hide something," Huey said, sounding peeved.

"Okay, fine, but if you insist on me going, call her and tell her to meet us at Dale's place. I might as well enjoy the meal if I have to spend my time with a reporter when it's not my idea." Chili grabbed her keys and stopped at the doorway. "I'm taking the stairs so meet me downstairs."

"Yes, ma'am," she said, and saluted. When Chili left she looked at her father and blew out a long breath. "You think I'd be interested in that?"

Huey gazed at her and seemed the most relaxed she'd seen him in weeks as he strolled to the elevator.

"Enjoy it while you can, Daddy. Enjoy it while you can."

❖

"Can I tell you something?" Sam asked when they were in Chili's car headed to lunch.

"I could tease you over that question, but I'll pass. What's on your mind?" Chili turned out of the parking lot and headed toward the Quarter but took a turn into the driveway of an abandoned building three blocks away. Once they'd stopped moving she turned to face Sam. "Can I go first again?"

"Sure." Sam put her hand out, and Chili took it and kissed her fingertips.

"Don't think because I can tell tales when it's called for, that I'll use those talents to get something over on you."

"You're like a mind reader. At first I thought you were trying to ditch me, but you played Daddy like a pro back there. We're not only going to lunch, but it was at his insistence." Sam traced Chili's lips with her index finger. "I don't want to get all crazy on you, but the thought of you with someone else makes me insane."

"Don't think of me with someone else, and keep your sanity. I won't lie to you. Up to now I've had plenty of women in my life, but they haven't really been in my life. More like plenty of women have been in some of the hours or days of my life, but no one that has meant enough for me to want to extend our time together." She kissed Sam and waited until she opened her eyes. "That in no way describes you."

Sam replaced her finger with her lips and kissed her. "Thank you for the therapy session, but let's get going before Maria teases me any more than she's going to already."

Maria was waiting for them, and when they joined her, Dale

came out of the kitchen and sat with them during the appetizers and had them all laughing until he excused himself and Chili followed him back. She figured she'd give Maria the freedom to talk about her to Sam, and she could be totally honest.

"That girl is smitten with you, Chili," Dale said when the kitchen door swung closed. "Hurt her and I'm going to feed you something disgusting without your knowledge, but I'll be happy to tell you about it a few weeks later."

"Are you going out there and tell her the same thing?" She accepted a piece of coconut cream pie from one of the workers, even though lunch was still coming.

"Did you not hear when I said she was smitten with you? I mean, how many times in your life do you get to use the word 'smitten'? Hearing it now should stick in your head like 'Oh, my God, I just ate a rat burger.'"

"Got it—smitten," she said, and laughed. "Think they're done talking about me?"

"They still have their heads together and your date keeps looking in this direction," the woman who'd given her the pie said.

"She's not packing up to leave, is she?" Chili asked, and stayed glued to the stool she'd picked instead of going to sneak a peek herself.

"It's more like they're planning the rest of your life and what color nose ring will look best on you."

"Okay, time to get back, and whoever lets my brother feed me rat for any reason is in for an ass-whooping. Don't say I didn't warn all of you."

❖

"How was she?" Maria asked, the second Chili left the table. "Does it live up to all the hype?"

"I'm not giving you anything on that, so change the subject." Sam took a sip of her wine and glanced at the door where Chili had disappeared, wondering what Dale was saying about her.

"No need. You look so relaxed the quality of the orgasm is written all over you," Maria said with a smug smile. "My suggestion now is to buy her one of those sturdy choke collars with a matching leash to keep her under control."

"Is that the secret to your relationship?"

"Yes, and Danielle knows better than to take it off too. She was a lot like Chili when we met, but a few dates later I had her eating out of my hand. It's all in the execution."

Sam laughed and shook her head. "More like you threatened execution and thankfully Danielle fell in line. Never mind that she loves you more than anyone else in the world, including your mother."

"Please, my mother wouldn't know love if it came up and chewed her leg off."

"Okay, bad example," she said as she watched Chili appear through the door again. "And please, don't embarrass me before dessert."

"I wouldn't dream of it," Maria said, her smug expression back.

"Should I come back later?" Chili asked when she sat down.

"Why'd you quit?" Maria asked.

"I took the day off, Ms. Poplin, and this is the angle you're taking to make me say otherwise?" Chili asked as Sam took her hand under the table. "Slow news day?"

"Sam called me and told me you quit. You calling Sam a liar?"

Chili gazed at her before turning her attention back to Maria. "Well, if Sam said it, it must be true, only I'd beg a favor and ask you not to report anything on the subject. Only I know Sam didn't call you and tell you that. I'm happy at the firm, and I'm even happier with people I work with, so I'm not going anywhere. If there was ever anything wrong, it's like in most families. Stuff comes up and it's handled."

"Okay, I'll take your word for it if you promise me something in return."

"Name it," Chili said as the servers put their lunch down.

"Don't make Sam sorry for anything at any time."

"I know you two are friends, and I could just tell you something to shut you up," Chili said, and Sam squeezed her fingers.

"But you're not," Maria said.

"But I'm not is right. On the record that counts with you, Sam is safe with me. I know the difference between someone like Sam and Paula."

"You've kicked that trash to the curb, I hope?" Maria asked.

"A long time ago, so don't worry about your best friend. Besides, my brother threatened some kind of rat dish if I don't behave and treat Sam right." They all glanced down at their plates and shivered before laughing.

The rest of lunch was filled with more humorous banter than probing questions, and Sam enjoyed herself with two of her favorite people. It was a relief that Maria liked Chili and vice versa. And that Dale approved of them as well was a good sign for their future.

As they were leaving, Maria asked both of them out to dinner one night when they could both attend so Chili could meet Danielle. On their way back to the office Chili took a detour and stopped at Sam's place and turned the ignition off.

"You can say no, but we're working late tonight and after that you're having dinner with your father," Chili said, to start whatever she was after.

"So a quickie after lunch?"

"Maybe later, when I don't want to take the long scenic

road," Chili said as she removed her keys from the ignition. "But between then and now, I want to kiss you so you'll know how much I'm going to miss you."

"You think I'm turning that down?" Sam didn't wait for Chili to open her door like she usually did and headed upstairs.

They never made it past the front door since Chili pressed her up against it and, true to her word, kissed her until she wanted to beg for more. "Come on," Chili whispered in her ear as she held her. "We need to get back."

"You want to leave now?"

"No, but it's going to be hard to explain why we were gone for lunch all day." Chili held her tight enough that her feet left the ground.

"I only thought this was going to be a long day when you handed out assignments today," she said as she kissed Chili's cheek. "It's going to be torturous now."

"I'll let you deal with your father's duck-hunting trip and who to invite as a way to get your mind off how cruel I'm being by making you go back to work."

"I thought he made all those arrangements."

Chili laughed as she let her go. "After one election you'll realize that your father likes to enjoy some of the events with as little personal input as possible. Just think, though, that if you plan it, you get to pick who you hunt with, if you decide to go."

"Daddy says you always hunt alone and that you must concentrate on ducks the whole time, since you win every year. What the hell do you do with all those ducks, since you don't cook?"

"I give them away to families who live close to where your dad's land is."

"If you're going to be concentrating on that, I might stay home and wait until you get all that out of your system." She headed to the bathroom in her bedroom and smiled when Chili followed her and sat on the bed.

"You're new, so let me explain something to you," Chili said loud enough for her to hear. "If you work for Huey, this thing is not a choice. You're going, and you're going to have a smile on your face the whole time like you're excited to be there."

"I'm sure if I ask him real nice he'll let me slide." She finished in the bathroom and came out to sit on Chili's lap.

"You can try it, but don't get mad when he shoots you down faster than one of those ducks flying around out there." Chili laughed in a way that made her believe her dad wouldn't let her out of something she really wasn't looking forward to.

"Can I hunt with you?"

"Can you keep my secrets?"

"What, you have a special duck call or something?" Sam asked as she sandwiched Chili's face between her hands.

"You'll have to wait and see," Chili said as she stood with her cradled in her arms.

"I'll think of something to wheedle it out of you."

"I'm not that easy."

When Chili kissed her for the last time before opening the door to leave, she wanted to say she was that easy, but duty called. "We'll see."

Chapter Thirteen

They ended up working late every night until Election Day. While most of the office was out making sure people were getting to the polls, Sam stayed and helped Chili at Virgil's headquarters. The only time they left was to follow Virgil to his precinct to control the media that had hooked on to the election for no other reason than nothing else was going on.

"You want to take the precinct a mile from here?" Chili asked Sam as the polls closed. The results would be posted at each place in less than an hour.

Sam was waiting for a more personal celebration since they hadn't had much time alone since their first night together. "No problem. Want me to grab the one about five miles from that?"

"No. I just need you to get the numbers from that one, then come back." Chili never looked up from her screen as she spoke, which made Sam want to kiss her to get her attention. She would've, but today wasn't the moment to freak out the staff.

"You need anything while I'm out?"

"Just come back, since no one here comes close to having as cute an ass as you do," Chili said, finally glancing up and winking at her. "Be careful and take Paul with you so you don't have to park too far away. If you get mugged we'll have to delay our evening."

"Why?"

"You'll have to come down and bail me out of jail when I kill Paul for letting that happen."

Sam laughed. "I'll be fine, and I'm sure Paul has better things to do than to babysit me."

"He can either go with you or babysit me. You want to ask him which he prefers?"

She ran her hand along Chili's back as she left, and Paul watched her do it but didn't say anything until they were on the way back with the good news that Virgil had won the area closest to his house by a four-to-one margin.

"I'm happy for you," Paul said.

"With the results we just got, I'm happy too."

"That's not what I'm talking about. She's changed since you've been around, but it's a good change, so I'm happy for both of you. Please take care of her. She's an incredibly special person."

"Thanks, and I promise not to let you down since you'll follow her out the door if I mess up." She turned the corner and was surprised by the crowd that had shown up while they were out. They'd parked close to the precinct, but here, they had to find a spot three businesses down. Thankfully they were all closed and she wouldn't get towed.

"Don't worry. Chili's not going anywhere."

Sam wrote their numbers on the big board Chili had erected close to Virgil's office, and theirs was the only one that was so lopsided. The rest were incredibly close, but once everyone had come back from their results, Virgil had won by five votes. It was so close that Chili sent them out again to recheck their numbers, but it added up to the same thing again, and it was the lead story that night on the news.

Virgil had taken on a career politician and won. Granted, it was by a razor-thin margin, but Chili had told him that one vote more than the other guy when only two people were in the race meant that you won. "We need to claim victory, so you ready to go?" Chili asked Virgil as they sat in the office watching the numbers scroll at the bottom of the screen during the primetime show on right before the news. Sam sat by the phone and nodded at what Chili was saying.

"I'm thinking of giving you whatever car you want off my lot for this," Virgil said as he slapped his hands together. "I'm just kidding, but hell if you didn't get this done. When we met I had my doubts because you made me over like a woman on one of those shows, but you were right."

"All you have to do now is keep your word and wear that orange tie sparingly. When all those guys at the capital start kissing your ass, remember our first conversation when I asked you why you were running." Chili shook his hand and smiled her attention in the other room. When Sam looked in the same direction Chili was, she saw Virgil's mother in an outfit she was sure the cameramen coming would put on the air.

"You got it, and you have a job for life when it comes to any other office I decide to run for."

"Maria and a couple of the other stations are here," Sam said after Paul waved to her and pointed at the front door. "Before we go out, you need to do one more thing," Sam told Virgil as she held out a bag to him. Inside was the pink tie they'd bought him on that first day. "You promised."

"That I did, and I want to thank you two for everything. You were here almost every day, and Chili told me this is the first campaign you've worked from beginning to end. We have that in common, but I have a feeling you're going to get much better at it than me."

They stayed in the office and let Virgil and his family enjoy the moment, both of them laughing when Maria waved and held up five fingers and mouthed the word "wow." Virgil was right in that this was her first campaign as a full-time employee, but as excited as Virgil was right now, his opponent had to be equally frustrated. All he'd have had to do was get a few more of his friends out to vote and that edge would've gone in his favor.

"Think the guy who ran against us will be crying for the next six years?" Sam asked Chili as Virgil took questions from the reporters huddled around him.

"First, he's going to be crying for a recount, so we have to beat him to the punch and ask for one first." Chili took her phone out and brought up her contacts, and Sam wasn't surprised she had the registrar's office on the list. It didn't take long, but after a short conversation Chili had the guy's promise that they'd seal the machines within the hour and open them in the morning as soon as they called the other campaign to invite them to be there.

"Now that these guys are interested in a party, can I interest you in a late dinner at my place?" Sam asked.

"What's on the menu?" Chili looked at her, and the corners of her mouth turned up slowly into what Sam considered a sexy smile.

"It's one of my personal recipes," she whispered, which made Chili have to lean in a little to hear her.

"Sounds interesting and I'm starving. Only thing is we can't leave until your pal over there and her competition finish asking all the stupid questions they can think of."

"If you're trying to get me to hate the media, it's working," she said, and laughed along with Chili. "This was a small campaign compared to most of the ones we're involved with, and we've had a bunch of late nights. What's it going to be like when we start Rooster's campaign?"

"It's not going to get any better, so we'd better get good at finding ways to carve out some time, or I might have to quit and go work for Daisy." Sam felt Chili's hand slip into hers, but no one noticed since they were focused on Virgil, who was doing an admirable job of answering questions.

"I'm glad you said that," and Sam was, because it made her more sure of her growing feelings for Chili.

"Why?" Chili asked, her face still really close to Sam's.

"You don't strike me as the sappy I-miss-you type, and it makes me glad you aren't any different from me. I am the I-miss-you sappy type, in case you didn't get what I meant."

"I understand perfectly," Chili said as she threaded their fingers together. "Any progress on your dad's pet project?"

"The invitation list is sitting in your inbox at the office. Once you approve of everyone going, we'll put everything in the mail." She pressed closer to Chili, and it made her look forward to doing the same thing naked. "When Daddy retires, can we change the annual duck-hunting soirée into something that doesn't involve guns?"

"As long as it doesn't involve a day at the mall shopping for anything, count me in."

"I bet there's plenty at the mall I can interest you in," Sam said as Chili pushed off the doorjamb and walked to the front of the room. When she went to complain she saw her father patting Chili on the back, probably for another check in the win column. "This is getting ridiculous."

"Well?" her father said when he hugged her.

"Well what?"

"How'd you like it?" Huey held her at arm's length with a huge smile on his face, while Chili stood behind him. "This is your first step in taking over for the old man, and I was hoping you love all this as much as I do."

"Give me a few more years in the trenches before you start talking about me taking over anything. The only thing happening on the top floor is budget considerations and billing, and I'm not ready to give up the hands-on stuff yet." Chili must've heard that part since she laughed and understood the true meaning behind the statement. She was ready for some hands on.

"Don't worry about that. I'm not anywhere ready to retire, so you'll be stuck with Chili for a while longer."

"Yippee," she said into her father's ear since the crowd had started clapping as Virgil wrapped up his comments.

"I'll leave you and the team to finish up here. After a few days to decompress from all this, we start on getting Rooster elected to the Senate." Huey hugged her again and turned and hugged Chili as well. She knew from growing up with him that her father wasn't one to linger at a party like this.

"Beth," Chili said, once Huey had shaken hands with everyone from where they were to the door. "Can you wrap up here and make sure the newly elected official gets home okay?"

"Will do, and we'll close this out tomorrow after everyone gets to the office. We should be able to deliver Virgil his road map to Baton Rouge late tomorrow."

"Road map?" Sam asked.

"Chili started this when she came to work for the firm. We put together a recap of the campaign so each candidate can use it to make changes the next time around."

"Doesn't it also give them the opportunity to change firms with a blueprint of all our moves?" Sam asked, glancing back at Chili.

"You'd need Chili and the rest of us to make the playbook work. At least that's what Chili threatens them with when she hands the information over," Beth said, and winked. "Up to now no one's ever challenged her on that claim."

"All right, stop talking about me like I'm not here. Sleep in tomorrow, Beth," Chili said as she went to congratulate Virgil once last time. "Your place or mine?" she whispered in Sam's ear when she was done.

"Yours," she said as she shivered. "I gambled and packed a bag before I headed over here."

"Smart girl."

"More like a teachable one."

Sam had repeated something Chili had told her on their first day together, making Chili laugh. "Why do I have a feeling I'm the one who's going to be in school from now until I die?" Chili opened the back door for her and walked her to her car.

"I like the sound of that."

❖

Sam parked next to Chili's car and saw that Chili was sitting on her trunk waiting for her since she'd beat her there. Chili took her bag and shouldered it so she could hold her hand on their way to the door. For some reason, the move made Sam think of the future and what it held with Chili. It was way too early for her to be craving nights like this.

"What are you thinking so hard about?" Chili asked as she unlocked the door. "Are you tired? I can do sandwiches and we can head to bed if you want."

"You don't mind?"

Chili dropped her bag and held her. "I'm happy you're here, and that's good enough."

"If anyone heard you say that, you'd lose your hound-dog card," Sam said as she hooked her fingers in the belt loops at the back of Chili's pants. "Being this domestic isn't going to kill that wild streak of yours, is it?"

"I'm sure you'll keep me at my best, so don't panic because I'm willing not to ravish you right this second. There's always the morning." Chili led her into the kitchen, where they found a light pasta dish and a note from Dale. "Even if I calm down a little, you'll still eat well."

"I hope Dale doesn't mind sharing you," she said as Chili kissed the side of her neck.

Chili's hands went to her waist and she lifted her onto the counter. "I think Dale needs to find his own girl, and I think I want to change my mind about the whole quickie concept."

"Oh yeah," she said as Chili's hands went up the sides of her legs under her dress.

Chili reached her underwear, and instead of taking them off, Chili ran two fingers along the elastic around her leg and got underneath so that only her fingertips were touching her. She was wet, and when Chili moved her fingers up and found her hard and ready, both of them exhaled. "Think you can find a little energy before we call it a night?" Chili asked.

Chili kept her fingers moving from her opening to her hard clitoris, making her wish they were both naked. She pushed Chili's jacket off and unbuttoned her shirt until she reached her belt. Since Chili hadn't stopped, she was uncharacteristically uncoordinated as she fumbled as if her fingers had swelled along with other parts of her body.

Sam snorted as Chili laughed when she yanked hard enough to make her take a step forward. "Stop laughing or I'm going to rethink the concept of the quickie too," she said as the damn belt finally came undone. "As a matter of fact, the quickie at lunch a couple of days ago is enough of that for this week."

The campaign had kept them hopping, but every few days since their first night together was all they could stand before they found themselves naked and hungry whenever they had a break in their day. It wasn't ideal, but Chili had stayed all night a few times, and if they woke up early enough they spent a little more time with each other.

"I can't help if you're addicting enough for me to need a fix every so often," Chili said as her pants dropped to the floor. She stood still as Sam took a pair of scissors out of the knife block and cut off the briefs she was wearing. "I guess I know what to ask for when my birthday rolls around." Chili unzipped her and seemed to enjoy it when she wiggled the dress down so Chili wouldn't have to move her hand.

"You know what I've never told anyone ever?" she asked as Chili released the clasp of her bra with one hand, taking the straps down with her teeth. When she asked the question, though, Chili seemed to freeze in place. Even her fingers stopped moving.

"What?" Chili asked, the word coming out in a whoosh of air.

"Fuck me," she said, and her words brought Chili back to life. She lowered her head and bit Sam's mound gently through her panties. Chili was kinder to her underwear as she removed them impatiently.

After they were both as naked as they could get without breaking totally apart, Chili lowered her head again and put her mouth on her. Sam rested her feet on Chili's back and grabbed the sides of Chili's head to keep it in place. Eventually they'd have to talk about what had scared Chili into stillness, but right now she felt too good to think too hard about anything.

"Oh, Jesus," she said as Chili flattened her tongue and pressed it down hard as she slipped her fingers in. She let go and bucked her hips up and into Chili's face, but nothing stopped Chili from finishing what she'd started. They had all night but the end came quick, and she pulled Chili's hair to make her stop. Her orgasm had been so good she'd become too sensitive to touch.

Chili straightened up and kissed her so she could taste herself on Chili's lips. She laughed when Chili let her go for a moment and put a fork in the dish Dale had left and handed it to her so she could pick her up and carry her upstairs to bed. They shared most of it, alternating bites as she fed Chili while she straddled her on the bed.

"You want to tell me what scared the hell out of you earlier in the kitchen?" she asked, mentally fussing at herself for her lack of control. Nothing scared someone who'd never been in a long-term relationship more than asking them what scared them about being in a long-term relationship.

"Can I plead the fifth for now? I promise you'll have an answer before too long."

"Do you promise?" Her brain was ordering her to shut up, but her heart was in charge for the moment.

"You'll be the first to know," Chili said as she took the bowl from her and put it on the nightstand.

"I'm sorry if I'm being a pain in the ass."

"Baby," Chili said, referring to her by a term of endearment, something she'd never done. "I wouldn't call it pain, more like a kick in the pants, and I'm beginning to think I've needed that for a very long time."

"This is the perfect time. Any sooner and someone would've snapped you up and I would've lost out."

"Sam, you're one of a kind, and I would've been the one who'd be poorer if you hadn't taken a chance on me."

Sam lay down and rested her head on Chili's shoulder. "That was the sappiest I've ever heard you, and I'd like to hear more of it."

"Pretty soon I'm going to get so soft no one'll hire me," Chili said, but put her arms around her. "You're turning me into a teddy bear."

"It'll take a lifetime of coddling to make you soft, sweetie, so I wouldn't worry about it."

"Are you applying for that position?"

"Positions are becoming my specialty, so you'll have to wait and see," Sam said as she pushed her knee between Chili's legs.

❖

Chili let Beth and Sam deliver Virgil's report and finish their work with him. In her opinion he'd be happy in the position he'd won, but you never knew what politics would eventually do to people. Whether it was for reelection or another office, Virgil was theirs for life. That she was sure of.

She went up to meet with Huey so they could review what they wanted to take on. For the first time she sat across from him and had no real fervor about what came next. All she could think about was Sam. What surprised her most was that she didn't care, so it was time to learn to balance her life or lose the parts that had defined her for so long.

"So Rooster is next?" Huey asked, oblivious to her lack of attention. "Then what? How many contracts do you think we can take on and not sacrifice service?"

"All I concentrated on was Rooster, but it's time to put out feelers, because we've got the governor's race here and in Mississippi. That's been nothing but a cluster here, so if we're taking on a client I'd like final say on who we work for. I've had enough of dealing with the assholes who've been in there for the last couple of election cycles."

She closed her book and stared at the picture of Sam he had on the credenza behind his desk. It was time to go fishing and get her head straight.

"Sounds good. You okay?" Huey asked, as if he'd just noticed she wasn't her usual aggressive self.

"I'm fine." She smiled to try to get him off the subject. "My trip with Dale is coming up in a few days, so I'm giving everyone time off until I get back."

"Are you sure? Rooster isn't the most patient man in the world. He's going to want us twenty-four seven. I take that back. He's going to want you twenty-four-seven, and nothing else will satisfy him."

"The staff got a car salesman with no political experience elected to the Louisiana State Senate, and they sacrificed their holidays and any New Year's plans to do it. It was no easy task, and getting Rooster to leapfrog that asshole who's in the seat now is going to be an even more Herculean task, so I'm giving them some rest before they're here twenty hours a day." She stood up and smoothed her pants. "Fire me if you want, but I've already told them they could go."

"Is every conversation we have going to take the same

track?" Huey stood and rested his weight on his hands after he laid them flat on his desk. "We had a talk about Sam because I thought it was necessary," he said as pushed up, and he walked toward her. "I thought our relationship could survive what we both know is best."

"I love you, Huey, and nothing is going to change that, but it doesn't always mean that I like you very much. You can't throw that out there and not think it's going to change things, or make me act differently when I'm here." She put her hand up to stop him from coming closer. "I thought we were on our way to becoming partners, but you proved me wrong."

"So your resignation wasn't bullshit?"

"I'm not quitting. If you want me out, then tell me to go, but it's you who's going to end our working relationship."

"Unless you find a reason to be here I'm not going to force you to stay, but I'm not going to fire you either."

"I have found a reason to be here, and it's the only reason I'm not leaving."

"I'm guessing it's not me and our relationship?"

She laughed at Huey's attempt at humor. "It's a big part of it, but not exactly the whole enchilada."

"You giving up all that catting around?" He moved close enough to put his hand on her shoulder. "I haven't seen you with a Candy in a while."

"I could've learned discretion."

He laughed and slapped her on the back. "You do surprise me all the time, so good for you." Before she left he held his hand out and waited for her to take it. "Whatever changed your mind about leaving after my disrespectful behavior, make sure you're absolutely ready to take on the responsibility before you make any promises you're not ready to keep."

She took his hand and nodded. "We'll have a talk about it when I get back, but what changed your mind if we're talking about the same thing?"

"Carla, Rooster's wife, and I had a nice chat at the chamber lunch before it turned into a food fight. After that I learned two things."

"I can't wait to hear this."

"I should've learned to love again since Rooster seems so happy, and I shouldn't stand in the way of anyone's happiness when it's staring me in the face. You and Carla were right. When it's not my own life and what I want out of it, then it's not my decision to make."

"I'll give Carla all the credit for that one, but sometimes you are an important part of someone's happiness."

"We've been in politics too long, my friend. We can talk in this gibberish and still understand each other."

She laughed and nodded. "We get any better at it and we could run for office."

"Fuck that. We're better off as kingmakers than slaves to the confinement of office."

"And you say I have a way with words."

"I do, and I have a way to remove your spleen with a dull, rusty spoon if you fuck up any relationships here. And before you think that's gibberish, I'm dead serious about it. We understand each other?"

"I understand you, boss, and I keep a dull, rusty spoon in my desk, so don't think you'll have to hunt for one if I forget this conversation."

CHAPTER FOURTEEN

On their last day in Cabo San Lucas, Sam laughed at Chili and Dale's antics. They were constantly teasing each other, but they'd never left her out of their fun. It had only been four days, but it was enough time to get Chili to relax to the point that Sam felt she'd made it over every barrier Chili had erected around her heart. What really made her happy was that Dale was her greatest ally on that front. His acceptance of her in what had been up to then his time with Chili, and his joy for what they'd found together, made her extremely happy.

They'd spent the day on the boat Chili had hired for their trip, and the siblings had caught enough fish to keep the restaurant in entrees for months. When Chili had said Dale always picked fishing, she didn't realize that's all they did every day of their vacation, but it had been fun watching them enjoy each other's company. Throughout their last day, Dale, she thought, had overindulged so he'd have a good excuse to leave them alone for the night, and when they docked again, she kissed his cheek before he left to sleep off some of the hangover that was surely coming.

While she was getting ready, Chili went to his room to make sure he was okay, and Sam had ordered room service for him for later. She'd offered for them to stay and take care of him, but

Chili refused and stripped to jump into the shower. Once she was in there Sam finally took off her robe and got dressed.

Chili came out of the bathroom with a towel wrapped around her waist, and that made Sam want to stay in for other reasons than to take care of Dale, but she was ready for some fun on the town and Chili had promised another memorable date. "You look a lot sexier with a tan, babe," she said when Chili stopped to study her from head to toe as she spoke.

Chili struck a pose with her fists on her hips and held it for a few seconds before she started laughing. "I'm glad you think so, but you're the good-looking one in this relationship."

She'd laid out Chili's clothes after she'd gotten dressed first, wanting to surprise Chili with the outfit she'd bought the first day they got there and she'd picked shopping instead of fishing. The top and skirt she wore would only make future appearances when they were on vacation, and she'd bought it to give Chili some incentive to invite her along again. Now that she had Chili's attention, she crossed her legs and the slit at the side of the long skirt made the material fall away, showing plenty of leg.

"You sure you want to go out?" Chili asked as she dropped the towel.

"Yes, so get dressed and behave. You promised me a date, and after tonight I have to go back to a weekend in the marsh chasing ducks with a bunch of air-bag politicians, so I'm holding you to it."

"You drive a hard bargain," Chili said as she started to get dressed. "And you might not find that duck thing as bad as you think."

"Actually I've been thinking about that." She stood and pulled the drawstring on Chili's light cotton pants and tied it off. "You don't really strike me as the big-gun hunter type."

"When duty calls I can adapt." Chili pulled the linen shirt over her head and held her hand out to her. They weren't really leaving the resort for dinner, but they did plan to go into the city later on for some entertainment.

"I'm looking forward to seeing that in action."

"Speaking of action, are you sure you don't want to stay put tonight?"

Sam stopped and put her arms around Chili. "A light dinner and a little dancing will warm me up."

"Okay," Chili said as her hands wandered a little.

"That will make me warm, but when we get back I should be hot."

"I need to write that down," Chili said as Sam grabbed her by the wrists to help her keep her resolve to go out.

"You won't have time to take any notes tonight."

"Good thing I have a good memory."

Sam smiled as Chili opened their door. "Your ass ain't all that bad either."

❖

When they got back, Chili and Sam were the only two with a great tan, which made it hard to deny they'd spent their break together. If Huey was pissed by that fact, he hid it well. That was until he came down and called Sam upstairs with some lame excuse about needing her help for an upcoming debate tour for a few of the offices up for grabs in the coming three years.

The one good thing was that he'd gotten Chili the one meeting she most probably wanted when it came to the governor's race. Sam had seen the excitement in Chili's face as she left to meet with Kathleen Bergeron's people and knew from some of their conversations that getting Kathleen elected would mean a major shift in policy in Baton Rouge. Their governor now was as far right as you could get without actually falling off the scale, and some of his ideas he'd pushed into becoming law had done extensive damage to a lot of entities dear to Chili's heart, like higher education.

"Did you have a nice time on your short vacation?" Huey asked as they sat in his conference room with a lot of paper in front of them that outlined some new strategies he wanted to implement.

"Very relaxing, thanks for asking. It was good to get away from all this for a little while."

"Did you talk to Chili while you were gone?"

"I get enough of Chili the poll-vaulter Alexander while I'm here. I didn't need that on vacation," she said with some heat. She didn't add that she couldn't really get enough of the laidback Chili who couldn't keep her hands off her while they were away from judgments like Huey's.

"That doesn't sound good," he said as he cocked his head to the side, as if trying to figure out what was behind her outburst.

"Maybe I'm not over her dressing me down on my first day."

"Okay, then before we get started on this, I wanted to talk to you about a few things. This might be a good time to cover them." Sam turned her chair to face him and waited for him to speak. "I'm thinking about moving you up here after Rooster's campaign. Once that's over and with the experience you gained during Virgil's campaign, I think it's time for you to take a more active role in running this place."

She paused before answering, since her father's declaration was like throwing down a dozen land mines, and she didn't want to step on any. "If I weren't your daughter, would you promote someone this fast? And please be honest."

"No, but you *are* my daughter, and like it or not, you're my only heir."

"That's true, but it's going to take a lot more than Rooster and Virgil to qualify me for your office, so if you're asking me, I respectfully decline."

He put his hand on her knee and took a deep breath. "When I started this firm I had about that much experience myself, but I took the chance anyway. I did it because your mother and I saw that working for someone else wasn't the way to make the changes in the world that we wanted. If you don't want to move up to this floor, maybe it's time to move you up on the floor you're on."

"What do you mean by that?" she asked, thinking he'd move her in with Chili. That was a win if he decided to be that progressive.

"You taking over for Chili."

"How about we drop this and wait at least another year before we talk about it again. You and Mom might've been in a place where you could start at the top with no experience, but I know myself. I'm not at that point yet."

"Fair enough," Huey said as he squeezed her knee and leaned over to kiss her cheek. "How about you get back to your cubicle and we'll discuss this later. When Chili gets back I'm sure she'll be ready to go."

"Let's work a little, and I'll get in line when she gets back."

"You okay?" he asked, when she took a few deep breaths.

"Peachy," she said, but what she really wanted to do was run out and find Chili in case her father was planning an ambush for some reason.

❖

They went down together when the call came that Chili was on her way back after having closed the deal. The first thing Sam heard was the whispers of how Chili couldn't fail in a room full of women, straight or not. It was almost a known fact to these people that Chili could bend lines when it came to any woman she set her sights on. After they'd gotten together, joking like this had made Sam angry that people still saw Chili that way, and it upset her that Chili had enough wins in that area to have gotten the reputation in the first place. Sometimes the fun of the past was hard to compete with.

She concentrated instead on the truth that she wasn't the only woman to share a bed with Chili, but she did plan to be the last one. And when the object of her thoughts walked out of the stairwell door, the smile on her face meant there might've been a little flirting going on. Not enjoying the jealousy that overtook her senses, Sam decided to follow her father back upstairs for a little while.

That stay had been short-lived when he loaded her down with his new project and sent her back to her cubicle. She decided to take the stairs even with the box of papers and smiled when she heard footsteps headed her way. "You look way too smug, baby."

"That's the hazard of being this good," Chili said before she stuck her tongue out at her. "I finally get to have fun when it comes to the governor's office."

"How much fun did you have this morning? I know the meaning of that smile you had when you got back, and it means nothing but trouble." She gave up her box when Chili took it from her and didn't put up a fight when Chili stood a step down from her and kissed her.

"I was smiling because I was thinking about celebrating with you later."

"Uh-huh," she said as Chili put the box down and her hands went to her butt.

"I'll prove it to you when we get out of here," Chili said, and kissed her again. "Let me run this down for you, and then I have an appointment with your father."

"I should warn you he's in a strange mood."

"What are you talking about?" Chili moved slowly enough for her to keep up.

"First he offered me his job, I think, and when I turned him down, he offered me yours."

"I'd be okay with that," Chili said, and laughed.

"Sure you would."

"Are you denying I do a great job under you?" Chili said, and Sam's face got hot. "If this door was locked you'd be in big trouble, but until then…" Chili kissed her again, long and hard enough to make Sam want to take the rest of the day off. "While I'm still your boss, get to work and make sure you read the report."

"Rooster's dad didn't abandon him, did he?"

"I don't know, but it might be in the report. Ask an uninformed question now, and I reserve the right to put you over my knee and spank you."

"That'd be something your little minions won't ever forget."

"Neither will you when we try it out later at my place," Chili said, and Sam's face got hot again. "Go on before that blush stays put. I'll be down in a little while."

❖

"What's on your mind?" Huey asked when she closed the door to his office and sat down. "Before you start, though, let me repeat what a great job you did with Kathleen. I might even move downstairs and help you with this one."

"Thanks, but I wanted to talk to you about something else."

Huey stood and walked around his desk and sat next to her. "What can I do you for?"

"First, I want to apologize for keeping something from you. I not only work for you but I consider you a friend, and I don't especially like deceiving you in any way. Not that I did, but I'm sure you'll see it that way."

"You're seeing Sam after I asked you not to."

"I am, but it's not what you were worried about."

Huey leaned back and tapped his fingertips together. "What do you think I was worried about?"

"That I'd play her like I have in the past. Forget about ancient history. It's not why I asked to see you." She'd practiced this talk the night before and on the way back from her meeting. "I want your blessing."

"Blessing?" Huey repeated the word, making it sound like she didn't understand it. Then he was as blunt as ever as he spoke his mind. It didn't go quite as she'd planned, so she thanked him for his time and went downstairs to try and lose herself in the work. She didn't come up for air until Sam called her to remind her what time it was with the cute line about pinching nipples.

They'd have to talk about what had happened, but not tonight. It could wait for tomorrow, even though they'd be stuck at a duck hunt. "I'm in the hunt now, but I feel more like a sitting duck," she said when she got in her car. "Not a good thing with the number of guns that are going to be around tomorrow."

❖

An eerie mist rose from the water of the bayou the group the firm had invited was standing around while the hunting guides put small boats in the water. Everyone was wearing camouflage and shivering as they stood there holding shotguns and trying to stay warm until some of the eager media personnel noticed them. The news crews always came, wanting to get pictures and sound bites for the Saturday-night news cycle.

The annual event was the perfect launching point for those new to the game and those back for another taste of the power apple, and while most everyone outside the state probably didn't think much of the sport, duck hunting was a Louisiana tradition. Huey had enjoyed this tradition with his father and grandfather, so this was his opportunity to mix a little business with his passion.

On most mornings during the season Huey could be found on this boat launch introducing his hobby to as many people as were willing to sign up. Only this time not only interns and new friends were waiting for the sunrise; the group consisted of mayors, senators, representatives, councilmen, and other elected officials wanting to build alliances over the weekend.

Chili finally had no choice but to get out of her car, so she walked over with a beautifully tooled weapon that looked almost too fancy to fire. She held it casually with the double barrels cracked open as she made her rounds, greeting their guests as a few of the female staffers from different places followed her around chatting about different things, like they were trying to attract her attention.

More than one politician held up a fist full of money when the cameras weren't trained on them as Chili and her growing entourage joined them. The land was privately owned and stocked by Huey, so more than one bet was made along the way as to who brought back the most ducks. Limits didn't apply for the day, and Chili's record hung in the balance.

"Chili, you ready to go?" Only a few people were left milling around on the dock when Jean Pierre found her. The young man who was Huey's groundskeeper always gave her a ride out to her blind that he'd built to her specs when she joined the firm.

"Ready as ever, good luck everyone," she said as she got in his aluminum-hulled boat most Louisianans called a Joe boat. "Let's get going before one of these guys fills my ass with buckshot. Did you get out there last night?" Jean Pierre had gladly kept the secret to her hunting success and always stocked her blind with whatever she asked for.

They both zipped up their camouflage jackets when he pulled the starter on the small, quiet outboard and pushed away from the dock. It was still dark, but Jean Pierre had grown up in the marshes they were headed into and could've gotten there blindfolded if necessary.

Spending time with him, Chili had come to appreciate the beauty of the wetlands and had joined the growing consortium of concerned citizens fighting to save them. Coastal erosion was the new buzzword in politics, but for people like Jean Pierre, it was a fight to hang on to his heritage. That his priorities had become hers as well was something that made Jean Pierre want to please her more. But it wasn't lip service. She'd tried to work the fight to save the coast into every campaign and had convinced whoever they were representing to be passionate about it.

"I sure did, and thanks for the case of Gentleman Jack. You know I won't tell Huey what you're doing out there with or without the bribe, right? Though if he finds out, you'd better start running. That's my advice."

"You'd think he would've asked before now why I always insist on hunting alone, but like in most things, Huey doesn't ask when he really doesn't want to know the answer."

Jean Pierre killed the engine and glided the last fifty yards until the flat bow hit the small patch of land that her blind was situated on. "Pick you up at ten so stay put."

The heel of her Timberland boot disappeared into the mud when she stepped out, and she tried not to grimace. She didn't mind the outdoors, but when it started to ooze into her shoes it was a bit much to take. "Stay put, he says. Where in the hell do you think I'm going to wander off to?"

"I know you, smart-ass, you bore easily, so cool your jets until I get back."

"Relax. The only way I'm going swimming out here is if a Starbucks magically surfaces out of the water," Chili said, and laughed as she stepped on the small deck outside her blind. "Anyway, you should be nice to me or I won't warn you to ride clear of Councilman Smith's blind if you don't want to get your eye shot out. It's not sunup yet, but he's already sauced."

"How'd that one get past you? He can't be too effective in representing the masses if he's drowning his sorrows in Jack every minute of the day. Granted, it's my favorite, but not while I'm working."

"Into every life a little alcoholic must fall, I always say. Bert is mine, and that's my only defense. It's also why he'll find me representing whoever decided to run against him next year. Hell, I'll even do it for free if they're decent enough." She waved to him when the engine started up, and he headed farther into the marsh. "Don't forget my order before you come back for me," she yelled, getting a wave of acknowledgment in return.

❖

A makeshift flap of heavy tarp was the door to the blind, and Chili pushed it aside to get out of the cold. She was sure this was the only one on the property with a butane heater, crude wooden floor, cot, CD player, and a refrigerator stocked with champagne and orange juice. On top of that sat a tray of fruit and some muffins and sandwiches.

The place was warm since Jean Pierre had come by earlier and turned up the heat, so she left her muddy boots at the entrance, rested the gun in the corner, and hung up her jacket. With socked feet, she headed for the cot and put on the headphones. Vivaldi's *Four Seasons* lulled her into closing her eyes and crossing her feet at the ankles. This was as relaxed as she ever got and how her visitor found her when she pulled open the flap.

Chili opened her eyes when she heard the footsteps getting closer, since her guest hadn't bothered to remove her shoes. "If I get mud on my socks I'm going to be pissed." She removed the headphones and laced her fingers behind her head, wanting to admire the shapely butt when Sam bent over to unlace her footwear.

"It'll make us even then." A boot landed close to Chili's with a thud after Sam threw it across the cramped space.

"Even on what?"

"If those idiots in their ridiculously tight hunting clothing had gotten any closer to you this morning on the pretense of getting a look at your gun, I was going to have to do something about it. Their flirting and your not doing anything about it pissed me off, so we're even." Sam threw her other boot with the same precision, leaving her in a pair of fleece socks.

Chili chuckled at the straight posture and the balled fists. Charm alone wasn't going to defrost the mood. "I wasn't flirting—"

"The hell you weren't," Sam shot back.

She dropped the headphones to the floor and swung her legs around and stood. "Flirting is buying a woman flowers and serenading her from the street even though I can't sing worth a damn." Their shared memory relaxed Sam into opening her hands and falling back against her. "Flirting is wanting to find ways to get the girl of my dreams to kiss me every time I have her within reach. Flirting is also allowing said woman into my inner sanctum to enjoy the morning."

"Do many women fall for this bullshit?"

"One bouquet of flowers got me noticed." Chili put her fingers on the zipper of Sam's coat and pulled. "The serenade outside her window got me a picnic."

"All that was my idea, you know."

Chili unfastened a few buttons of the flannel shirt Sam had ordered for this thing after she'd asked for some input. "You're the idea part of the team and I'm the one who executes the plan, so pay attention." She slipped her hand in and placed it on Sam's stomach.

A little scratch made Sam laugh and reach up to put her hands behind Chili's head. "She sounds easy."

"Easy?" Chili laughed, and as always, Sam joined in. "She's my boss's daughter and she made it anything but easy, so don't rewrite history, pumpkin."

"You did look cute with the mariachi band, at least until you started singing." Sam removed Chili's hand so she could turn around and face her. "This place is cozy, which makes me think dark thoughts."

"If this place had a history I would've had Jean Pierre tear it down and start over, so don't worry about dark thoughts." With ease, she picked Sam up and carried her to the cot. Outside, the sound of gunfire started as the first fingers of dawn started to paint the cloudy sky. "I usually spend this time listening to classical music to drown out the barrage of gunfire and squealing water fowl, and that's as sexy as it gets. I keep telling you my past isn't as X-rated as everyone makes it out to be." She stopped by the cot but stood there enjoying the way Sam's legs were wrapped around her waist. "Today though, I thought I'd spend it showing you how much I care about you."

She knelt, seating Sam gently on the cot, and finished with the buttons to reveal a camouflage bra. "I see you dressed appropriately in case you have to sneak up on a duck in your bra."

"I saw it in that stupid catalog you gave me and thought you'd like it," Sam said, as if trying to sound aggravated.

Chili kissed the swell of one breast. "I love it, sweetheart." The button of the pants came next, and Sam helped by lifting her rear so Chili could take them off. The matching bottoms had little flying ducks embroidered on the waistband, making Chili smile. "This is as close to any ducks as I want to get today."

Their first kiss was filled with the passion that had been building from the moment Chili had seen Sam that morning and had ignored her because they were working. It was always like this for Sam from the first time she had let Chili through her front door, and the reason she'd tried to resist her. Chili had a way of stripping away her inhibitions and awakening a need she didn't know she had. Given a chance, she was sure Chili could make anyone a glutton when it came to sexual desire. If she moved on she'd die of starvation.

Chili kissed her and squeezed her ass to the point it almost hurt, and she instantly got wet. Sam's moan was long and deep, and even though she wasn't as experienced as Chili in this arena, she was beginning to master the art of weaving snares, as Chili would've described it. Without effort, Sam had spun a trap that Chili had more than willingly stepped into months ago.

"I want you to do something for me," Sam said when they broke apart.

Chili came closer when she flexed her legs and pulled her in. "What do you want?"

Sam ran her fingers through Chili's light-brown hair before pulling away to stop Chili before she was able to claim another kiss. "Control."

Simple concept, but from their time together, control was something Chili never gave up too willingly. Sam planned to change that today and knock down the final barrier between them. "What do I get in return?" Chili asked.

Instead of answering her, Sam placed a finger on Chili's forehead and pushed her back until she was sitting on her heels. To keep her in place Sam put her foot on her chest and applied enough pressure to keep Chili from moving. The game had begun, whether Chili realized it or not, and Sam was so far ahead there was no catching up.

"Take it off," Sam ordered, the throbbing between her legs making her voice husky. Not wanting to give in too easily, Chili took her time with her sock, smiling at her, and Sam recognized her facial expression. Having Chili's warm fingers on her skin was making her breathe faster. "You can wipe that grin off your face," she said as Chili put her hand farther up her leg, as if it needed to be there to finish her task.

"What grin?" Chili asked, as her smile widened.

"The 'if I bide my time she'll be begging me in no time' grin," Sam said as she pressed her toes harder into Chili's chest. "It's not going to be that easy today."

Chili nodded and looked down as if not convinced of that claim, then froze when her sock came completely off. The first time Sam had figured out this particular weakness of Chili's had been after a late-night work session in Chili's office when Sam had slipped off her pumps.

Red toenail polish was Chili's kryptonite. She even admitted after their third date that to her it was the epitome of femininity. Chili worked a little faster to get the other sock off and lowered her eyes to admire her pedicure.

"Whatever you want, it's yours," Chili said as she put her hands behind her back.

"Stand up," Sam leaned back with no intention of removing anything else just yet, "and take your shirt off." Chili's hands went immediately to work and started unbuttoning in rapid succession. "Slowly," she said, not wanting to cut her show short.

Chili's nostrils flared and her hands stilled altogether. From the look in her eyes Sam could tell that an internal war was taking place inside Chili. She wanted to object, and Sam could think of only one way to tip the outcome in her favor. She sat up again and reached behind her to the clasp of the bra. The cups slid down a bit when the back came undone, but Sam held it in place. Chili's nostrils flared again, but now Sam guessed it was from a different kind of frustration.

Sam had never thought of herself as beautiful and desirable until the first time she saw this same raw hunger in Chili's face. The sight had awoken the woman Sam had always wanted to be, and that was the only woman in Chili's bed. That self-realization hadn't come until after the first night they'd slept together.

As slowly as she wanted Chili to go, Sam reached for one of the straps and dragged it off her shoulder. Chili studied her every movement, and Sam smiled at the way Chili's fingers twitched, almost as if she was also fighting the need to touch her. The next strap came down just as slowly, and Sam made eye contact before the garment fell away.

Naked from the waist up, Sam leaned back again and ran a hand from her stomach to underneath her right breast. Chili's head fell slightly forward in defeat as Sam pinched her already-hard nipple, making her release a hiss of pleasure as she repeated the move on the other nipple.

"I believe I asked you to slowly take off your shirt," she said, and ran her tongue along her top lip.

Her hands returned to her stomach as Chili began unbuttoning her shirt again. It was agonizing for Sam to watch, but Chili finally finished, leaving the heavy cotton garment hanging open. Underneath she wore a tight, sleeveless T-shirt for extra warmth, so it was time to speed things up a little. "Take it all off," she demanded, and Chili was almost instantly naked from the waist up. Sam licked her lips again at the sight of Chili's more-than-obvious need for her since her nipples looked hard enough to chip ice.

"Tell me, baby, are you wet?" Sam asked.

Chili closed her eyes and took a deep breath in an obvious effort to center herself. "Are you?" Chili asked.

"Do you want to stop?"

Chili's eyes flew open. It seemed that stopping now was most definitely the last thing Chili wanted, and the authority in Sam's voice knocked the last of the fight right out of her. "No, I don't."

"Answer my question."

"I'm very wet," Chili admitted softly, "and it's because of you." The added comment came close to making Sam give in, but she hadn't finished playing yet.

"Take your pants off and let me see."

This time Chili remembered to go slow, unbuttoning her cargo pants and letting them drop to her ankles. It left her in a pair of tight white briefs, and the sight of them made Sam jut her chest out a little. The underwear wasn't coming down without help so Chili followed them all the way to the floor, bending over to pull them off, along with the pants and socks. When she straightened up, she faced Sam naked, waiting for her next set of directions.

"Do you know what I've been thinking about since the last time we were together?" Sam sat up again, set her feet on the floor, and waited for Chili to acknowledge the question. Chili stayed quiet but shook her head, though she seemed to bristle with a restless energy. She reminded Sam of a thoroughbred in the starting gate. Given permission, Chili would explode with a burst of power until she crossed the finish line.

"I've thought about how your mouth feels on me." Sam parted her knees and crooked her fingers, and Chili came closer. With a feather touch she ran her fingers along Chili's sex, her confidence growing at what she found.

Chili was very wet and more than ready. "I've been dreaming about your tongue right here." Sam leaned back on one hand and slipped the hand she'd used to touch Chili under her waistband and between her legs. When her fingers reappeared, they were glistening. "About how I can taste myself on your lips when you kiss me after you're done, and how it makes me want to do it all over again when I do."

Rocking on her heels, Chili swallowed hard. "Sam, please."

"Hold me," Sam said softly. She stood up and sighed when Chili engulfed her in her arms. The sweetness of the act despite how turned on Chili was made Sam come close to telling her how she felt. Fear of Chili bolting kept her quiet though, and she stayed silent as Chili moved to pull off the last barrier between them. "On your knees, Alexander," Sam said.

This time Chili didn't argue at the command, and Chili groaned when Sam painted her lips with her wet fingers. When she was done they kissed again, and Sam let her mouth relax into a brief smile when again Chili conceded control, letting her lead this dance. When she couldn't take it anymore, Sam pulled on Chili's hair again, leading her head lower down her body.

Like she was presenting Chili with a gift, she lay back,

prepared to give Chili what they both wanted. "Make my dreams a reality." Weaving their fingers together, Chili lowered her head and ran her tongue through the wet heat. Sam was more than ready, and immediately her hips began to rock. Before she really wanted, she held Chili's head in place and gave her last order. "Now, baby, now."

Chili's fingers slid easily in and took away the last of her resolve and restraint. Sam exploded against Chili's mouth and fingers with a yell that scared the few ducks that had obviously landed outside. The feeling of possession was so complete that Sam was sure she'd never give this part of herself to anyone else, even if Chili was too afraid to completely commit to her.

"Wait," she panted, when Chili began to start again.

Chili moved up and rested her head on Sam's abdomen for a minute. The position seemed to give her the courage to speak. "Do you know what *I* think about?" The uncertainty was so evident in Chili's voice that Sam let go of one of her hands and ran comforting fingers through her hair.

"You can tell me anything. It's okay."

"I think about our stolen moments like this, and they're not enough for me." A tentacle of fear reached into Sam's chest, and she thought the pain of it would constrict her lungs until she couldn't breathe. She had no choice but to look down when Chili's head came up and she gazed up at her.

"What do you mean?" If this was it, she wanted to know so she could make a clean break. It would take forever to get over it, but that was better than hanging on to something that would never grow past this point, no matter how good Chili made her feel when she touched her.

"I want all of you, Sam. I love you, and I want all of you for as long as you'll have me. No more sneaking around, and no more hiding how I feel about you."

"You love me?"

"I didn't think I'd ever be good at this, so I'm sorry if I've made it so you don't believe me. I do, and I love you enough to have talked to Huey about my intentions for his little girl."

The tease had its desired effect, and Sam laughed. "You talked to my father and there was no bloodshed?" She pulled on Chili's fingers, wanting her to move up and hold her. "What happened?"

"We'll get to that later. Right now we need to finish our talk." Chili moved to the jacket she'd hung up and took something out of the pocket. "I've been a coward up to now in not telling you what you mean to me. Remember what I said at my parents' anniversary party about not ever finding what they had?" Chili asked, and she nodded as Chili knelt by the bed. "I have, and I never could've imagined being this happy, but I am because I love you."

"I love you too," Sam said as she sat up and pressed their foreheads together. "I didn't say it before now because I thought you'd freak out."

"You're a smart woman, and I want to spend a lifetime learning anything you want to teach me." Chili held up a small velvet box. It creaked when she opened it, and Sam held her breath when she saw the ring. "Maybe after enough elections where we put the right folks in office, we'll get to marry legally in Louisiana, but until then I want you to take this as a sign of my love for you. There'll be no other in my life because I've found perfection in you." Chili took it out and held it close to her hand. "Will you marry me?"

"Yes," Sam said, not believing she was awake and that this was happening. Overwhelmed, she started crying, surprised when Chili joined her not only on the bed but in the show of emotion. "I guess I should be honest and tell you that from the first day I started and stepped into the jungle, I began my own campaign strategy."

"Did it work out for you?"

"My father thinks I'm immune to your charm."

Chili laughed and moved her hand down to slap Sam gently on the butt. "You are. I've never had to work so hard at getting someone's attention. For the longest time during Virgil's campaign, I thought it'd take begging for you to have a cup of coffee with me."

"I just wanted to make sure when I fell in love with you, you'd be good and snagged, baby. This was one campaign with a lifetime term limit, so I wanted to win by a landslide." She placed her palm on Chili's cheek and kissed her. "I love you, and I can't wait to start a life with you for real."

"Can we do something now about your wanting me?" Chili's low voice cracked when Sam's fingers closed around one of her nipples.

"I'd be happy to, if you tell me what my father said later, much later." It was the only words they exchanged until Sam wrenched a yell out of Chili. Sam figured if this was how they spent their time during this gig, the duck hunt would remain a proud company tradition.

❖

Jean Pierre pulled out his paddle and moved farther into the pond when he heard Chili yell in an uncharacteristically high-pitched tone that sounded a lot like Sam's name. He laughed but wasn't taking any chances that today would be the day Chili finally fired that beautiful gun she'd bought as a prop for this hunt every year. At his feet lay a pile of ducks that would more than assure that Chili would keep the record for making the most kills.

It was their secret, and the money Chili won off the fools that bet against her went to duck and other wildlife conservation in the state. Chili thought it was hilarious, and the folks who ran that organization considered Jean Pierre one of their best donors since Chili made him put his name on the donation.

He was happy for his old friend, and he was sure she'd gladly give up any title, duck hunter or otherwise, to keep the smile on Sam's face. When he'd dropped Sam off earlier she didn't seem to mind walking through the mud, but after hearing how they were spending their morning, he understood why.

CHAPTER FIFTEEN

A year later

Paul entered Chili's office and dropped a copy of the *Washington Post* Business section on her desk. "The new sign on the building made the news."

The room had been rearranged the week after the duck hunt and now housed a large partner's desk at its center. The side closest to the windows always held a vase of roses that Daisy delivered with a few jokes for Sam. Chili glanced down at it after she rolled the last of Rooster's campaign plans away and covered the boards with fresh paper.

The special election had been fast and furious after Fudge's resignation from office for a number of improprieties that went beyond hiring prostitutes, and while the race had gotten crowded and ugly, Rooster had won it without a runoff. "Must've been a slow news day," Chili said.

"You always say that, and it's never true," Paul said as he rolled his eyes. "The other big news is you received a dinner invitation from the new senator and his lovely wife as a way of thanking you for all the help, and to congratulate you on the wedding. They were sorry they couldn't get to New York for the festivities, but he wanted to let you know you and Sam were in their thoughts. He also said he forgives you for taking a long weekend away from the craziness of campaigning since it was for such a good reason. Carla sent a shotgun as a wedding gift from both of them and said you'd understand."

Sam answered when she joined them. "She does understand that, but we should be celebrating the fact that Daddy didn't think it was necessary when he walked me down the aisle. And tell Rooster we accept." Her arms went around Chili's waist as she leaned against her.

"It's still kind of shocking that he gave me his blessing that day I went up to see him, instead of punching me in the nose," Chili said as she kissed the top of Sam's head.

"You never did finish telling that story," Sam said as she sat on the sofa the staff crammed on when they had meetings.

"Your father's got a good sense of humor. He just said he wasn't blind, but after some reflection on the romance vote, he figured it was a smart move to endorse me in my campaign to get you to marry me."

Sam laughed and shook her head as if knowing that's exactly what her dad would say. His blessing had been important to both of them, but especially to Chili. This place and Sam were her home, and she hadn't wanted to lose either.

Sam picked up the paper and tapped on the color shot of their new sign. "This is great free advertising. Alexander, Pellegrin, and Morris has a nice ring to it."

"I guess this means you won't be giving up duck hunting anytime soon, huh?" Paul asked Chili.

Chili joined Sam on the sofa and pulled her onto her lap. "After winning the heart of the most beautiful woman in the world and Huey's wedding gift of a partnership, it's safe to say I'm not going anywhere."

"It's a good thing too," Sam said, and kissed her. "Daddy knew he didn't need a shotgun to get you down the aisle, but keeping you in line is another story."

About the Author

Ali Vali is originally from Cuba and has frequently used many of her family's traditions and language in her stories. Having her father read adventure stories and poetry before bed when she was a child infused her with a love of reading, which is even stronger today. In 2000, Ali decided to embark on a new path and started writing.

Ali lives in the suburbs of New Orleans with her partner of thirty years, and finds that residing in such an historically rich area provides plenty of material to draw from in creating her novels and short stories. Mixing imagination with different life experiences makes it easier to create the slew of characters that are engaging to the reader on many levels. Ali states that "the feedback from readers encourages me to continue to hone my skills as a writer."

Books Available From Bold Strokes Books

Courtship by Carsen Taite. Love and Justice—a lethal mix or a perfect match? (978-1-62639-210-6)

Against Doctor's Orders by Radclyffe. Corporate financier Presley Worth wants to shut down Argyle Community Hospital, but Dr. Harper Rivers will fight her every step of the way, if she can also fight their growing attraction. (978-1-62639-211-3)

A Spark of Heavenly Fire by Kathleen Knowles. Kerry and Beth are building their life together, but unexpected circumstances could destroy their happiness. (978-1-62639-212-0)

Never Too Late by Julie Blair. When Dr. Jamie Hammond is forced to hire a new office manager, she's shocked to come face-to-face with Carla Grant and memories from her past. (978-1-62639-213-7)

Widow by Martha Miller. Judge Bertha Brannon must solve the murder of her lover, a policewoman she thought she'd grow old with. As more bodies pile up, the murdered start coming for her. (978-1-62639-214-4)

Twisted Echoes by Sheri Lewis Wohl. What's a woman to do when she realizes the voices in her head are real? (978-1-62639-215-1)

Criminal Gold by Ann Aptaker. Through a dangerous night in New York in 1949, Cantor Gold, dapper dyke-about-town, smuggler of fine art, is forced by a crime lord to be his instrument of vengeance. (978-1-62639-216-8)

Because of You by Julie Cannon. What would you do for the woman you were forced to leave behind? (978-1-62639-199-4)

The Job by Jove Belle. Sera always dreamed that she would one day reunite with Tor. She just didn't think it would involve terrorists, firearms, and hostages. (978-1-62639-200-7)

Making Time by C.J. Harte. Two women going in different directions meet after fifteen years and struggle to reconnect in spite of the past that separated them. (978-1-62639-201-4)

Once The Clouds Have Gone by KE Payne. Overwhelmed by the dark clouds of her past, Tag Grainger is lost until the intriguing and spirited Freddie Metcalfe unexpectedly forces her to reevaluate her life. (978-1-62639-202-1)

The Acquittal by Anne Laughlin. Chicago private investigator Josie Harper searches for the real killer of a woman whose lover has been acquitted of the crime. (978-1-62639-203-8)

An American Queer: The Amazon Trail by Lee Lynch. Lee Lynch's heartening and heart-rending history of gay life from the turbulence of the late 1900s to the triumphs of the early 2000s are recorded in this selection of her columns. (978-1-62639-204-5)

Stick McLaughlin by CF Frizzell. Corruption in 1918 cost Stick her lover, her freedom, and her identity, but a very special flapper and the family bond of her own gang could help win them back—even if it means outwitting the Boston Mob. (978-1-62639-205-2)

Rest Home Runaways by Clifford Henderson. Baby boomer Morgan Ronzio's troubled marriage is the least of her worries when she gets the call that her addled, eighty-six-year-old, half-blind dad has escaped the rest home. (978-1-62639-169-7)

Charm City by Mason Dixon. Raq Overstreet's loyalty to her drug kingpin boss is put to the test when she begins to fall for Bathsheba Morris, the undercover cop assigned to bring him down. (978-1-62639-198-7)

Edge of Awareness by C.A. Popovich. When Maria, a woman in the middle of her third divorce, meets Dana, an out lesbian, awareness of her feelings brings up reservations about the teachings of her church. (978-1-62639-188-8)